Andrew Melville

William Morison

Contents

ANDREW MELVILLE

BY

William Morison

CHAPTER I

INTRODUCTORY

While Andrew Melville has other claims on the lasting honour of his countrymen than the part he took in securing for Scotland the ecclesiastical system which has been the most powerful factor in her history, it may be held as certain that where this service which filled his life is disesteemed, his biography, if read at all, will be read with only a languid interest. It will be our first endeavour, therefore, to show that such a prejudice in regard to our subject is mistaken and misleading.

Melville, and all from first to last who joined in the Scottish resistance to Episcopacy, were persuaded that the controversy in which they were engaged was one not academic merely but vital, and that, as it was settled one way or the other, so would the people be left in a position in which they would be able to develop their religious life with freedom and effect, or in one which would incalculably cripple it. That is a contention which history has amply vindicated.

The best justification of the struggle carried on during the period from Melville to the Revolution (1574-1688) to preserve the Presbyterian system in the Church is to be found in the benefits which that system has conferred upon the country. It has penetrated the whole Christian people with a sense of their individual responsibility in connection with the principles and government of the Church; it has saved the Church from being dwarfed into a mere clerical corporation; it has laid for it a broad and strong basis by winning to it the attachment of its common members, and by exercising their intelligence, sympathy, and interest in regard to all its institutions and enterprises. It may be truly said of the Scottish people that their highest patriotism has been elicited and exercised over the religious problems of the nation; that they have shown more sensitiveness concerning their religious rights, liberties, and duties than concerning any other interest of their life; and that they have been more readily and deeply touched when the honour and efficiency of their Church was at stake than by any other cause whatever. How should an ecclesiastical system better vindicate its claim? Nothing so ennobles a people as the care of matters of high concern--such a care as Presbyterianism has laid on the Scottish people.

But it was not only the conviction of the excellence of their own economy that led the Presbyterians to maintain it at all hazards--it was also their fear of many tendencies in the rival system. They dreaded that the imposition of Episcopacy would ultimately undo the work of the Reformation, and bring the nation once more under the yoke of Rome. Here, too, history has justified them. Had it not been for the conjunction of the forces of the Scottish Presbyterians and the English Puritans during the reign of Charles the First, the designs of that monarch against the Protestantism of both kingdoms could not probably have been checked. The least that can be said with truth on this matter is, that the Protestantism of the country was gravely imperilled in his reign and in the reigns of his two immediate successors, and that the resolute attitude of Scotland counted more than any other one influence in preserving it.

Nor was it only the preservation of the freedom of the Church that was involved in the struggle. The cause of civil freedom was also at stake. 'True religion,' says a classic of the Scottish Church, 'and national liberty are like Hippocrates' twins--they weep or laugh, they live or die together. There is a great sibness between the Church and the Commonwealth. They depend one upon the other, and either is advanced by the prosperity and success of the other.' Where a people make a stand for spiritual liberty, they always by necessity advance civil freedom. Prelacy was bound up with the absolutism of the throne in the State as well as in the Church; Presbytery with the cause of free government and the sovereignty of the popular will, as declared in their laws by the chosen representatives of the nation.

But that is not the whole case for the Presbyterians. The opposing system was discredited in their mind by the policy by which it was promoted. It was a policy of coercion, of bribery, of dissimulation and artifice, of resort to every kind of influence that is intolerable to a free and high-spirited people. It was a policy that harassed the most faithful and honourable men in the Church, and preferred the most unscrupulous and obsequious to places of power. There was not one of those concerned in it, from the king downwards, who came out of the business with undamaged character. How could the Scottish Church but resist a system which it was sought to thrust upon it by such methods as these? If Melville's claims on our interest rested on no other ground than the services he rendered to the Church and to the nation in maintaining Presbyterianism in the land, that alone would make them good.

But Melville was not only the greatest ecclesiastical controversialist of his day; his name is pre-eminent in another sphere. He was the most learned Scot of his time; and our Universities never had a teacher within their walls who did so much to spread their reputation. His fame as a scholar not only checked the habit among the *elite* of Scottish students of resorting to the Continental Universities; it drew many foreign students to Glasgow and St. Andrews. His academic distinction has been overshadowed by his fame as the leader of the Church in one of the most momentous struggles in her history, but it was equally great in its own sphere. A Scottish historian--John Hill Burton--has sought, with a singular perversity, to belittle Melville as a scholar, and speaks of M'Crie as having ***endeavoured*** to make out his title to distinction in this respect from the natural ambition to claim such an honour for one of his own ecclesiastical forebears. The chapter which follows will show the value of such a judgment.

There is still another and a higher ground for our interest in Melville, namely, his massive personality. It is not so much in the polemic or in the scholar we are interested, as in the man. The appreciation of his character by his countrymen has suffered from his proximity to Knox. Had he not stood so close on the field of history to the greatest of Scots, his stature would have been more impressive. In historic picturesqueness his life will not compare with that of Knox, although it had incidents, such as his appearances before the King and Council at Falkland and Hampton Court, which are unsurpassed by any in Scottish history for moral grandeur. There were not the same tragic elements mixed up with Melville's career. His life fell on duller times and among feebler contemporaries. He had not such a foil to his figure as Knox had in Mary; there was not among his opponents such a protagonist as Knox encountered in Mary's strong personality. And yet it may be justly claimed for Melville that in the highest quality of manhood, in moral nerve, he was not a whit behind his great predecessor. He never once wavered in his course nor abated his testimony to his principles in the most perilous situation; in the long struggle with the King and the Court he played the man, uttered fearlessly on every occasion the last syllable of his convictions, made no accommodation or concession to arbitrary authority, and kept an untamed and hopeful spirit on to the very end. The work a man may do belongs to his own generation; the spirit in which he does it, his faith, his fortitude, to all generations. Melville conferred many signal and enduring benefits on his country: the one which transcended all others was the inspiration he left to her in his own rare nobility of character.

CHAPTER II

BIRTH--EDUCATION--YEARS ABROAD

'Fashioned to much honour from his cradle.'

Henry VIII.

Melville's birthplace was Baldovy, an estate in the immediate neighbourhood of Montrose, of which his father was laird. He was born on 1st August 1545--a year memorable as that of Knox's emergence to public life--the youngest of nine sons, most of whom came to fill honourable positions in the Church and commonwealth.

Montrose and the district around it early showed sympathy with the Reformed Faith. George Wishart was a native of Angus, and his influence was nowhere greater than there. The family seat of John Erskine--Dun House--was in the same vicinity, and he too by his warm espousal of Protestantism strengthened its hold on the district. The Baldovy family itself had been identified with the Reformed movement from the beginning. Melville's eldest brother, Richard, who became minister of Maryton, was travelling tutor to Erskine, and the two studied together at Wittenberg under Melanchthon. The Melvilles were intimate with Wishart; and Baldovy and Dun House were the resorts of other leading

spirits among the Reformers. In 1556 Knox was Erskine's guest when he
was preaching in the district, and his personal influence intensified
the attachment of the Melvilles to the cause to which they were already
committed.

Melville was only two years old when his father was killed fighting
among the Angus men on the field of Pinkie, a battle which made many
orphans; and in his twelfth year he lost his mother, when he was taken
by his eldest brother to Maryton Manse, and as tenderly cared for by the
minister and his wife as though he had been a child of their own. One of
the sons of the manse was James Melville, between whom and his 'Uncle
Andro' the most endeared affection sprang up. The two lived in each
other's lives and shared each other's work, alike as teachers in the two
principal Universities, and as leaders in the Council of the Church.
Corque unum in duplici corpore et una anima--so the elder, after the
younger's death, described their relationship.

Melville's scholarly bent showed itself early. 'He was a sicklie, tender
boy, and tuk pleasure in nathing sa meikle as his buik.' He began his
education in the Grammar School of Montrose, which had great repute, and
on leaving it he attended for two years the school in the same town,
founded by Erskine of Dun, for the teaching of Greek. It was in the
latter school that he learned the rudiments of Greek, in which he had
afterwards few equals anywhere, and none in Scotland. In 1559 Melville
entered the University of St. Andrews and joined St. Mary's College.
Aristotle's Works were the only text-books used; and Melville was the
only one in the University, whether student or professor, who could read
them in the original. He was a favourite of the Provost of his College,
John Douglas, who invited him often to his house and encouraged him in
his studies, and discerned in him the promise of distinction as a
scholar. 'He wad tak the boy betwix his legges at the fire in winter,
and blessing him say--"My sillie fatherless and motherless chyld, it's
ill to wit what God may mak of thee yet!"' Melville finished his

curriculum at St. Andrews in 1564, and left with the reputation of being 'the best philosopher, poet, and Grecian of any young maister in the land.'

It was common at that time for Scottish students on leaving their own Universities to seek, at the Continental seats of learning, a more abundant education than their own country could afford. We shall see that when Melville came to be at the head in succession of our two principal Universities, he considerably modified this custom. He conformed to it, however, in his own case, and the same year in which he closed his course at St. Andrews left Scotland to prosecute his studies abroad. The next decade was his Wander-jahre. He went first of all to Paris, whose University was the most renowned in Europe. There was a truce at the time between the Catholics and the Reformers in France; a large measure of toleration was allowed by the Government, and the principal Professors were Protestants. In Paris, Melville sat at the feet of some of the most distinguished scholars of the day: he read diligently in Greek literature; acquired a knowledge of Hebrew; and at the same time studied Philosophy under Petrus Ramus, the great opponent of Aristotelianism, becoming a follower of this daring innovator, whose system he afterwards introduced in the Scottish Universities.

From Paris Melville went to Poitiers, where he studied jurisprudence and was also employed as tutor in the college of St. Marceon. In the 'Diary' of his nephew, who was a great literary impressionist, and whose pages preserve for us the very 'form and pressure' of the scenes he describes, many incidents are related of his Continental life which disclose his character as a youth. During the third year of Melville's residence in Poitiers the academic quiet of the town was broken by the clash of arms. Civil war had broken out afresh in France, and Poitiers, which was a Catholic town, held by the Duke of Guise, was invested by a Protestant army under Coligny. Melville, as a foreigner and a Protestant, found himself in a situation where he needed to use the greatest caution to

escape the danger to which he was exposed. When the siege began the
colleges were closed, and he was received into the family of a prominent
citizen as tutor to his boy. There was a small party of the soldiery
quartered in the house, and one day their corporal, who had observed
Melville at his devotions, challenged him as a Huguenot, and threatened
to deal with him by martial law as one who might betray the town. With a
courage and an adroitness which were native to him, he at once turned
round on his assailant and repudiated his imputations; and seizing on
some armour that was lying by, donned it, and going to the stables took
the best horse by the head, as if to join there and then the ranks of
the army of defence, when the corporal, fairly nonplussed by the
apparent vehemence of his loyalty, begged his forgiveness. He had no
more trouble of this kind, but he never felt secure of his liberty, and
it was a comfort to him to know that he had a good horse standing in the
stable by which, if it should come to the worst, he could make his
escape to Coligny's camp. During the siege his pupil, a bright boy, to
whom he had become deeply attached, was killed by a cannon-ball which
penetrated the wall of his room and struck him on the thigh. Melville
was in the house at the time, and on entering the room the dying boy
embraced him and passed away with the words of the Apostle on his
lips--[Greek: didaskale, ton dromon mou teteleka]--'Master, I have
finished my course.' 'That bern gaed never out of his hart.'

On the siege being raised, Melville left Poitiers for Geneva, footing it
all the way in the company of a few fellow-students. If he was sickly as
a child, he gathered vigour in his 'teens and grew up a manly youth. He
was of short stature and great agility, high-spirited, brave, the
cheeriest of companions, full of resource in emergencies, and with an
artful humour by which he made his escape from many a difficult
situation incident to Continental travel at the time. On the journeys
from town to town on the way to Geneva he held out better than any of
his comrades, stepping along with no impedimenta but his Hebrew Bible
which he had slung at his side--the same Bible which he afterwards

'clanked' down on the board before the King and Council in
Edinburgh,--the freshest of the company when the day's journey was
ended, so that he 'wad out and sight' the towns and villages
whithersoever they came while the others lay down 'lyk tired tykes.' On
reaching Geneva he and one of his fellow-travellers, who was a
Frenchman, presented themselves at the gates together, when they were
challenged by the guard. 'The ports of Genev wer tentilie keipit,
because of the troubles of France and multitud of strangers that cam.
Being thairfor inquyrit what they war, the Franche man his companion
answerit, "We ar puir scollars." But Mr. Andro, perceaving that they
haid na will of puir folks, being alreadie owerlaid thairwith, said,
"No, no, we ar nocht puir! [though he admitted afterwards that they had
'but a crown to the fore' between them]. We haiff alsmikle as will pey
for all we tak, sa lang as we tarie. We haiff letters from his
acquentance to Monsieur di Beza; let us deliver those, we crave na
fordar.'"

In Geneva Melville received a warm welcome from Beza, who reigned there
in place of Calvin, and through his influence he at once obtained an
appointment to the chair of Humanity in the College. During his
residence in that city, which lasted for five years, he had the
opportunity of mingling with many of the first scholars of the age, and
of the leaders of the Reformed movement in Europe. After the massacre of
St. Bartholomew in 1572, Geneva was filled with Protestant refugees from
every Continental country. Never probably before or since has there been
found within one city such an assemblage of masters of intellect and
learning, or such a cloud of distinguished witnesses for truth and
liberty. In Geneva, Melville, like Knox, received much of his
invigoration for the work that awaited him on his return to his native
land.

His residence there was made still more agreeable by the hospitality of
a relative, Henry Scrymgeour, brother of his foster-mother. Scrymgeour

had left Scotland in early life to study law on the Continent, and after acting as tutor and secretary to several noble families in France and Italy, he had come to Geneva, and been appointed to the chair of Civil Law in the College. He had 'atteined to grait ritches, conquesit a prettie room within a lig to Geneva, and biggit thairon a trim house called "The Vilet."' In 'the vilet,' where Scrymgeour and his wife and daughter composed the household, Melville was always a welcome guest.

During Melville's ten years' absence on the Continent he had little correspondence with his friends at home, and towards the end, as they had heard nothing of him since he had left Poitiers, they began to fear that he had perished like so many others in the civil wars in France. A countryman, however, who had come to Geneva to see Henry Scrymgeour in order to invite him in the name of well-known friends of learning in Scotland to become a teacher in one of the Universities, brought back news of Melville's welfare and reputation, when his relations immediately wrote and urged him to return to his own country, and bestow his services as a scholar in raising the low-fallen repute of Scottish education. With great regret, and bearing with him a letter of commendation from Beza, in which this distinguished friend used these words--'the graittest token of affection the Kirk of Genev could schaw to Scotland is that they had suffered thamselves to be spuiled of Mr. Andro Melville, wherby the Kirk of Scotland might be inritched'--he left the city where, like Knox before him, he spent his happiest days. He arrived in Edinburgh in the beginning of July 1574.

CHAPTER III

SERVICES TO SCOTTISH EDUCATION-- PRINCIPALSHIP OF GLASGOW AND ST. ANDREWS

'He was a scholar, and a ripe and good one;
    ... Ever witness for him
Those twins of learning that he raised in you.'

Henry VIII.

It was in the interests of education, and for the purpose of reviving Scottish learning, that Melville had been induced to come back to his native land, and it will be convenient to devote a chapter to this subject before we consider the graver, more crucial interests in which he was destined to take a decisive part. He had not been many days in the country when Regent Morton offered him an appointment as Court Chaplain, with the ulterior view of attaching him to his patron's ecclesiastical policy. Whether having this suspicion or no, Melville declined the post. He had returned to Scotland for educational work, and he determined to wait for an opening in one of the Universities. Meanwhile he wished a little repose with the friends from whom he had been so long separated; and he went to Baldovy, where he was received with much affection. It was at this time that the attachment between him and his nephew was formed and consecrated by a kind of sacramental act on the part of the father of the latter--'I was resigned ower be my father hailelie into him to veak[1] upon him as his sone and servant,

and, as my father said to him, to be a pladge of his love. And surlie
his service was easie, nocht to me onlie, bot even to the fremdest man
that ever served him.'

[Note 1: Wait.]

So great was Melville's scholarly reputation by this time that, at the
General Assembly held a month after his return, the Universities of
Glasgow and St. Andrews put in competing claims for his services as
Principal. He decided in favour of Glasgow, on account of its greater
need; and at the end of October he left Baldovy, accompanied by his
nephew, to enter on his academic office. On the way two days were spent
in Stirling, where the King, then a boy of nine, was residing; and the
Melvilles saw him and were much struck with his precocity in learning:
'He was the sweitest sight in Europe that day for strange and
extraordinar gifts of ingyne, judgment, memorie, and langage. I hard him
discours, walking upe and doun in the auld Lady Marr's hand, of knawlage
and ignorance, to my grait marvell and estonishment.' James never lost
his fancy for discoursing at large and learnedly to the 'marvell and
estonishment' of his hearers. But it was to visit the King's illustrious
preceptor, George Buchanan, that Melville came by Stirling. The two were
kindred spirits; they were like in their love of learning, in their
scholarly accomplishments, in their passion for teaching, in their
political and religious sympathies, in the ardour and vigour with which
they maintained their convictions, in their valorous action for the
defence of civil and religious freedom. At this time Buchanan was
beginning the work which filled his closing years--his History of
Scotland. Seven years afterwards the Melvilles paid him another visit,
in Edinburgh, the account of which by the younger is one of the loci
classici of Scottish history. It contains, like the same writer's
description of the last appearance of Knox in the pulpit, one of the
most living pieces of portraiture in our literature: 'When we cam to his
chalmer, we fand him sitting in his chaire, teatching his young man that

servit him in his chalmer a, b, ab; e, b, eb, etc. Efter salutation, Mr. Andro sayes, "I sie, sir, yie are nocht ydle." "Better this," quoth he, "nor stelling sheipe, or sitting ydle, quhilk is als ill!"' Buchanan put the proof of his Epistolary Dedication to the King into the hands of Melville, who read it and suggested some amendments. 'I may do no mair,' said the worn-out veteran, 'for thinking on another mater.' When Melville asked what he meant, he replied, 'To die.' Leaving him for a little, the Melvilles accompanied his nephew, Thomas Buchanan, on a visit to his printer, whom they found setting up the passage of the *History* relating the 'burial of Davie.'[2] Its boldness alarmed them, and they asked the printer to stop the passage meanwhile. Returning to the house, they found him in bed, and, asking how he did, he replied, 'Even going the way of weil-fare.' His nephew then mentioned their fear that the passage referred to would so offend the King that the work would be suppressed. 'Tell me, man,' Buchanan answered, 'giff I have tauld the treuthe?' 'Yes,' replied his nephew; 'sir, I think sa.' 'I will byd his fead[3] and all his kin's, then!'

[Note 2: Rizzio.]

[Note 3: Feud.]

Melville needed a stout heart for the task that lay before him in Glasgow. The University, which had never been prosperous, being always starved in its revenues and undermanned, had declined so far that its gates had to be closed for lack of students; so that when he entered on the Principalship he actually constituted the whole Senatus in his own person. He began by training a number of young men as regents, the course of study embracing classics, mathematics, and mental and moral philosophy, in each of which he carried his class as far as the highest standards of any University in Europe; and in addition to these labours he taught all the theological classes. When the regents were qualified he specialised their subjects--a great reform on the old system, under which the students passed through the entire curriculum under the same teacher.

Melville's teaching was not confined to his class-hours nor to his professor's desk; he sat with the students at the college table, and in his table-talk gave them some of his best instruction. The fame of the University rose so rapidly under his *regime* that the class-rooms were soon crowded: 'I dare say there was na place in Europe comparable to Glasgow for guid letters during these yeirs, for a plentifull and guid chepe mercat for all kynd of langages, artes an sciences.'

In 1580 Melville was translated to the Principalship of St. Mary's College, St. Andrews. Mainly through his own exertions a new constitution for the University had just been framed and sanctioned by Parliament, in accordance with which that College was to be henceforth set apart for theological education. The reforms made at this time in St. Andrews went on the same lines as those effected in Glasgow.

Before Melville's time the study of Greek never went beyond the rudiments: Hebrew and other Oriental languages were not taught at all; and in philosophy Aristotle held exclusive possession of the ground. His reforms applied particularly to these branches of learning: Greek, Hebrew, and Syriac were taught according to the best methods of the age; and the Platonic Philosophy was introduced. M'Crie, who always speaks with authority on such a subject, describes the reformed curriculum as the most liberal and enlightened plan of study in any University, whether at home or abroad.

Melville continued in the Principalship of St. Mary's for upwards of a quarter of a century--from the close of 1580 to 1606, when he was summoned by the King to London, never to return to his native land.

In St. Andrews and Glasgow he had not only teaching duties, he presided

over the government of the University as well; and the same resolute
respect for law, which set him so stoutly against the King's tyranny in
the realm, made him a determined upholder of order in the University.
He was at once a fearless subject and a born ruler of men. When he
entered on his office in St. Andrews, some of the professors, chafed by
the reforms which he introduced, became insubordinate, but soon
succumbed to his authority; and more than once in Glasgow he quelled
riots among the students at the risk of his life. On one occasion, when
his friends urged him to condone an offence of a student of noble family
from fear of revenge, he answered, 'Giff they wald haiff forgiffness let
them crave it humblie and they sall haiff it; but or that preparative
pass, that we dar nocht correct our scholars for fear of bangstars and
clanned gentlemen, they sall haiff all the blud of my body first.'

In St. Andrews he was for some time Rector of the University as well as
Principal of St. Mary's, and in his exercise of civil authority in that
capacity he did more for public order than all the magistrates of the
burgh. At one time the inhabitants were greatly plagued by a bad
neighbour, the Laird of Dairsie, who had once been Provost, and who
resented his ejection from that office. On more than one occasion
associates of his, Balfour of Burley and others, had entered the city
during the night and committed gross outrages. One day the report
reached St. Andrews that Dairsie and his friends were approaching in
force to make an assault on the citizens. The magistrates were
panic-stricken; but on the report reaching the Rector's ears, he
immediately summoned the whole University together and organised a party
of resistance, placed himself at its head, bearing in his hand a white
spear (one of the insignia of his office), and by his prompt action made
the invaders glad to decamp.

During Melville's rectorship quarrels sometimes occurred between town
and gown, and in these he always showed himself jealous in regard to the
rights of the University. He had once a serious rupture with the

magistrates, on account of their unjust administration and their
rejection of eminent ministers whom he had commended for charges in the
city. Preaching in his own pulpit in the College of St. Mary's, he spoke
with such vehemence of their misdoings that he raised the town against
him. Forthwith placards were affixed to the College gates threatening
the Rector with dire revenge. Nothing daunted, Melville continued to
fulminate against the authorities--'with ane heroicall spreit, the mair
they stirit and bostit the mair he strak with that twa-eagit sword, sa
that a day he movit the Provest, with sear rubbing of the ga of his
conscience, to ryse out of his seatt in the middes of the sermont, and
with some muttering of words to goe to the dure, out-throw the middes of
the peiple.' Melville, instead of giving way to the irate magistrate,
had him brought before the Presbytery, when he expressed his regret for
disturbing the public worship, and craved forgiveness; and so peace was
restored.

The academic labours of Melville caused a great revival in Scottish
education. Not only did Scotland after this time keep her own students,
but foreign students began to attend her Universities. A few years
after Melville went to St. Andrews, names of students from all parts of
the Continent began to appear on the matriculation registers, chiefly of
St. Andrews, but of the other Universities as well. He gave an impetus
to learning not only within academic circles, but throughout the
country, as was shown in the great increase in the production of books
in all branches of literature and science. The period enriched the
nation with no names of literary genius, but the general intellectual
activity of the country made a great advance, Melville himself left no
permanent contribution to literature--his hands were too full of public
cares for that; and his entire literary remains consist of sacred poems
and fugitive pieces of verse in Latin. But he was very ready with his
pen, and served as a kind of unofficial poet-laureate. It is a curious
fact that on every occasion in the King's reign that called for
celebration, even at those times when Melville was on the worst terms

with James, an appropriate ode was forthcoming. He was a clever satirist, and it was a lampoon which he wrote on a sermon in the Royal Chapel at Hampton Court that was made the pretext for depriving him of his liberty.

Such were Melville's services to education and learning. Through all the stormy controversies into which he was plunged he never forsook his first love, but continued his work in our Universities up to the close of his career in Scotland.

CHAPTER IV

THE 'DINGING DOWN' OF THE BISHOPS--MEL-VILLE AND MORTON

'Who never looks on man
  Fearful and wan,
But firmly trusts in God.'

HENRY VAUGHAN.

We must go back to the year of Melville's return home, 1574, in order that we may review the supreme labours of his life. It was a time of confusion: Knox was dead, and the Church needed a leader to shape its discipline and policy in order to conserve the fruits of the Reformer's work. Two years before Melville's return, viz. in 1572, the electroplate Episcopacy--the Tulchan[4] Bishops--had been imposed on the Church by the Regent Morton. Up to this time the constitution of the Church had been purely Presbyterian. There was no office superior to that of the minister of a congregation. The Superintendents were only ministers, or elders appointed provisionally by the General Assembly, to whom such presbyterial functions were delegated as the exigencies of the Church required. They had no pretensions to the rank or functions of the Anglican bishops; they had no peculiar ordination, and no authority save such as they held at the pleasure of the Assembly.

[Note 4: A Tulchan was a calf's skin stuffed with straw placed near the cow to induce her to give milk.]

Side by side, however, with the Presbyterian ministry there still existed the old Roman Hierarchy, who had been allowed to retain their titles, the greater part of their revenues, and their seats in Parliament. The prelates had no place within the Church, their status being only civil and legal; and when any of them joined the Church they entered it on the same footing as the common ministry.

This was far from being a satisfactory or safe state of things. It had elements, indeed, which obviously threatened the integrity of the Presbyterian order; and it is little wonder that the Church was impatient of its continuance and eager to end it, to clear the Roman Hierarchy off the ground, and secure for its own economy a chance of developing itself without the entanglements that were inevitable to the existing compromise.

The financial arrangements that had been made at the first for carrying on the Church's work were unjust and inadequate. A portion of the third part of the benefices was all that had been assigned for the support of the ministry, and even this had not been fully or regularly paid, so that in many parishes the ministers' stipends had to be provided by their own people. In these circumstances the Church very naturally wished the ecclesiastical revenues of the country to be transferred to her own use, and she made the claim accordingly. But for this claim no party in the State would have resisted the sweeping away of the Hierarchy. The nobles, however, had set greedy eyes on the Church's patrimony, and so they became the determined opponents of this step. They could well have spared the bishops, but they could not forego the benefices, and to secure this plunder to the nobles was the main object of the Tulchan device. By this notable plan the benefices were taken from the old Hierarchy and bestowed on the nobles, who then conferred the titles without the functions on any of the clergy who could be bribed into compliance.

Morton, who was the chief supporter of the scheme, was notoriously avaricious--'wounderfully giffen to gather gear.' He hoped to enrich himself by it, and succeeded in doing so; but he had other motives. He wished--and this was always the main Governmental reason for the preference of Episcopacy--to keep the clergy under his control; and he sought also to please Elizabeth, on whom he was dependent for the stability of his own position, by bringing the Scottish Church into some degree of conformity with the Anglican.

The Assembly, while accepting the compromise had done what it could to safeguard its own constitution by putting it on record that it had assented to the continuance of the bishops only in their civil capacity, and in order to give a legal claim on the benefices to those who held them, and that it allowed the bishops no superiority within the Church over the ordinary ministers, or, at any rate, over the superintendents.

There is no doubt that it was only the hope, on the part of the Church, that she would secure a portion at least of her patrimony by it that reconciled her to this scheme. The ministers had little heart in the business, and the best of them did not conceal their dislike of the arrangement and their fear of the evils to which it would lead. It is easier to blame the Church for what she did than to say what she ought to have done. It would have been a more heroic, and probably a safer course, to refuse the compromise and at once to bring on the struggle with the Government which she had to face in the end. If Melville had been on the ground at the time, there is little doubt that one man at least would have had both the wisdom to recommend that course and the courage to pursue it.

The Tulchan system had only been in operation for two years when he came back from the Continent; but that was long enough to realise the Church's fears and to make her restive. The ministers who accepted the bishoprics became troublers of the Church, took advantage of their titular superiority over their brethren to push for a position of greater authority, and were more and more evidently the pliant tools of the Court. The Church, moreover, gained nothing in the way of a better provision for the ministry--the nobles seized the benefices and kept them.

On encountering the growing dissatisfaction of the ministers with his project, the Regent threatened the freedom of the Assembly, and put forward a claim on behalf of the Crown to supreme authority within the Church. There lay the crux of the situation, the great central issue in the controversy that was being thrust upon the Scottish people, that was to rend the nation for many a day, and that is not yet finally settled--Was the Church to be free to shape her own course and do her work in her own fashion, or was she to be subject to the civil government? Was the Church to be essentially the Church of Christ in Scotland, or was she to be the religious department, so to speak, of the Civil Service?

The first Assembly in which Melville sat met in Edinburgh in March 1575. Parliament had just appointed a committee to frame a more satisfactory polity for the Church, and the Assembly nominated some of its members as assessors to confer with it and report the proposals that might be made. At the same time it appointed a committee of its own, composed of its most competent and trusted men, to draft a constitution for its approval. This committee was reappointed from year to year; the result of its labours being the 'Second Book of Discipline,' which was laid before the Assembly and adopted by it at its meeting in the Magdalene Chapel, Edinburgh, in April 1578.

It was in the next Assembly, held in August of the same year, that the first blow was struck at the Tulchan Episcopate. This was done by a resolution brought forward by John Durie, one of the ministers of Edinburgh; but there is little doubt that it originated with Melville, who, although he had been home scarcely a year, had taken his place as the leader of his brethren, and by his teaching and personal influence had 'wakened up their spreits' to oppose the designs of the Court against the constitution of the Church. Durie's resolution raised the question of the scripturalness and lawfulness of the office of a bishop. In supporting it Melville made a powerful speech, in which he urged the abolition of the bishoprics and the restoration of the original Presbyterian order of the Church as the only satisfactory settlement of her affairs. The House resolved there and then to appoint an advisory committee to consider and report on the question, which committee reported against the office. No further step was taken at this time, the bishops being left as they were. At the next Assembly, however, held in April 1576, the committee's finding was adopted, and so far applied that all bishops who held their office 'at large' were required to allocate themselves to particular congregations.

The Assembly's decision was practically unanimous; its members were at one in wishing an end to the Tulchan scheme, and the people were of the same mind as the ministers. Against the ministers and people stood the Regent, the nobility, and all the clergy whose interests were threatened. Morton would fain have arrested the Assembly's action, but dared not; he could not afford at the time to drive the ministers into opposition, a powerful party of the nobles being hostile to his regency, and the combination would have shattered his government. His policy, therefore, was to manage the ministers for the accomplishment of his ends, and to attach as many of them as possible, and especially as many of the leaders as possible, to the Court. From the moment when he first met Melville he had the sagacity to perceive that this was the strongest man he would have to deal with: he accordingly did his utmost to secure Melville's support for the Government scheme. He offered him, as we have said, a Court Chaplaincy, and he would have made him Archbishop of St. Andrews on the death of Douglas. When he found him incorruptible by his favours, he tried to intimidate him. Calling him one day into his presence, he broke out in violent denunciation of those ministers who were disturbing the peace of the realm by their 'owersie'[5] dreams and setting up of the Genevan discipline; and on Melville turning the attack against himself and his government Morton flew into a rage--'Ther will never be quyetnes in this countrey till halff a dissone of yow be hangit or banished the countrey!' 'Tushe! sir,' retorted Melville, 'threaten your courtiers in that fashion. It is the same to me whether I rot in the air or in the ground. The earth is the Lord's: my fatherland is wherever well-doing is. I haiff bein ready to giff my lyff whar it was nocht halff sa weill wared, at the pleasour of my God. I leived out of your countrey ten yeirs as weill as in it. Yet God be glorified, it will nocht ly in your power to hang nor exyll His treuthe!' Sometimes, as here, words show a valour as great as doughtiest deeds of battle: they give the man who has uttered them a place for ever in the book of honour; they pass into the storehouse of our most cherished legends; and as often as crises occur in our history which make a severe demand upon our virtue, they are recalled to stir the moral pulse of the nation and brace it to its duty. No man in Scottish history has left his country a richer legacy of this kind than Melville.

[Note 5: Over the sea.]

Having failed with Melville, Morton found a ready tool to his hand in another minister of the Church, Patrick Adamson of Paisley. He was a man of some learning and eloquence and of great personal ambition, bent on climbing to a high place in the Church, and unscrupulous in his choice of means. At first he was a pronounced opponent of the new Church scheme, and often denounced it from the pulpit. His clever satire on the Tulchan bishops has never been forgotten--'There are three sorts of bishops: my Lord Bishop--he is in the Roman Church; my Lord's Bishop (the Tulchan), who while my Lord gets the benefice, serves for nothing but to make his title good; and the Lord's Bishop, who is the true minister of the Gospel.'

For some time Adamson cultivated an intimacy with Melville, who, however, never trusted him. Melville, ever shrewd in discerning character--'he had a wounderfull sagacitie in smelling out of men's naturalls and dispositions'--early saw that Adamson would prove a better servant of the Court than of the Church.

When the Assembly met in the autumn of 1576 it was reported that Adamson had been presented by Morton to the See of St. Andrews, and the question was put to him in open court whether he meant to accept it, when he declared he was in the hands of his brethren, and would act in the matter as they desired. The Assembly vetoed the appointment. Adamson, however, in violation alike of the Assembly's Act and of his own promise, entered on the See. The contempt his conduct awakened was universal, and was freely expressed even within the Regent's Court. One of the officers of the household, who had frequently heard Adamson come over the phrase, 'The prophet would mean this,' in his expositions of Scripture, remarked, on hearing that he had assumed the bishopric, 'For als aft as it was repeated by Mr. Patrick, "the prophet would mean this," I understood never what the profit means until now.' But to Adamson, who 'had his reward,' the titular primacy of Scotland was of more consequence than the respect of his countrymen: he retained his place in defiance of the Church, and was for many a day a troubler of its peace.

At the Assembly held in April 1578 a second blow was struck at the bishops: it was enacted that they should cease to be styled by lordly names, and that no more bishops should be elected. Two years later, at the Dundee Assembly of 1580, the Church took the final step against the Tulchan system by abolishing the Episcopate and requiring all bishops to demit their office and give in their submission to the provincial synods. The resolutions of the Assembly were carried without a single dissenting voice, and within a year the bishops with only five exceptions had surrendered their sees.

During the six years Melville had been the leader of the Assembly great results had been reached. The Church had gradually withdrawn from the Tulchan compromise, and had at the same time elaborated a constitution for itself on the basis of pure Presbytery. Mention has already been made of the adoption of this constitution--the Second Book of Discipline--in 1578. It is not necessary to describe it, as it is seen in its living embodiment in all the Presbyterian churches of Scotland to-day; though there is one important part of it which was never carried out, namely, the allocation of the patrimony of the Church to the purposes of religion, education, the maintenance of the poor, and the undertaking of public works for the common good. It enunciates the principle of the two jurisdictions--'the two swords'--which has played so important a part in Scottish history, and it protects the rights of the people in the election of their ministers. One significant difference between the Second Book of Discipline and the First may be mentioned--the abolition of the office of Superintendent. This office had been used as a handle by those who wished to introduce an order in the Church above the ministry; it thus lent itself as an inlet to Episcopacy, and so it was resolved to put an end to it.

The unanimity of the Assembly in the adoption of the 'Discipline,' and in all the steps towards the deposition of the bishops, was remarkable. The House never once divided. In all its counsels and labours Melville had the principal share, and it was mainly by his learning, by his energy, by his mastery in debate, by his unyielding attitude to the Court, that they issued as they did in the re-establishment of the Church on its original Presbyterian and popular basis.

James Melville has left us some charming pictures of the Assemblies of that period and of the private intercourse of its members. 'It was a maist pleasand and comfortable thing to be present at these Assemblies, thair was sic frequencie[6] and reverence; with halines in zeall at the doctrine quhilk soundit mightelie, and the Sessiones at everie meiting, whar, efter ernest prayer, maters war gravlie and cleirlie proponit; overtures maid be the wysest; douttes reasonit and discussit be the lernedest and maist quik; and, finalie, all withe a voice concluding upon maters resolved and cleirit, and referring things intricat and uncleired to farder advysment.'

[Note 6: Large attendance.]

In the inmost circle of Melville's friends were such men as Arbuthnot, Principal of Aberdeen, and Smeton, his own successor as Principal of Glasgow--both, like himself, eminent in learning; David Ferguson, minister of Dunfermline, the patriarch of the Assembly, and one of the six original members of the Reformed Church; and the four ministers of Edinburgh--all notable men--John Durie, James Lawson, James Balfour, and Walter Balcanquhal. At Assembly times he and his nephew met these brethren daily, for the most part, at John Durie's table. The group contained the very flower and chivalry of the Church. At their meals they discussed the incidents of the day's sittings, and their conversation was enlivened with many a pleasantry--it was always

Melville's 'form' at table to 'interlase' discourse on serious subjects with 'merry interludes.' When the company rose from table they held lengthened devotional exercises: in the reading of Scripture each in his turn made his observations on the passage; and we can well believe the estimate of some of those who were present, that had everything been taken down they could not have wished a fuller and better commentary than fell at these times from this company of ripe and ready interpreters of the Word. When the exercises were over, the brethren entered into deliberation on the causes to be brought before the Assembly, and came to an understanding as to the course they would pursue in dealing with them. Those who would come to the secret of the noble part so often played by the ministers of the Scottish Church in crucial periods of its history, will fail to find it where they leave out of account the inward correspondence which these men, by such fellowship, sought to maintain with one another and with the Master of Assemblies.

CHAPTER V

THE 'BIGGING UP' OF THE BISHOPS UNDER LEN-NOX AND ARRAN--MELVILLE'S FLIGHT TO ENGLAND

'To deal with proud men is but pain,
For either must ye fight or flee,
Or else no answer make again,
But play the beast and let them be.'

The Raid of the Reidswyre.

In March 1578, James, then in his twelfth year, assumed the government. In Morton he had had an adviser who was not friendly to the Church, but those who displaced Morton and brought him before long to the scaffold were its determined and avowed enemies. During the few years with which we have to deal in this chapter, the Government was directed by two men whose character and policy were detested by the nation, and who filled up their short tenure of power with as many exasperating acts of despotism as it was possible to crowd into it. The more prominent of the two, Esme Stewart, a kinsman of the King, cousin of his father Darnley, was a foreigner and had been trained in the French Court. He had a brief and inglorious career in Scotland. He had no sooner joined the King's Council than he became the master of its policy, being the first of the ***gratae personae*** who in succession established themselves in the Court of James and brought him under their control. There is little wonder that the boy-king, who had passed through the stern hands of George Buchanan and had spent his time for the most part with men of our austere Scottish character, should have felt the seductiveness of the gay foreigner 'with his French fasons and toyes.' Esme Stewart had not been long in the country before James began to decorate him with honours and enrich him with gifts of lands and money. He was created Duke of Lennox and made Lord High Chancellor, in which latter capacity he had the custody of the King's person--a pawn which in this reign was often decisive in the contest for political supremacy. He soon filled the Court with men of his own stamp. One of these, only second to himself in influence with the King, was another Stewart--James, the infamous son of Lord Ochiltree. Like his patron, James Stewart soon received high promotion, being made Earl of Arran.

Lennox had come to Scotland as an emissary of the French Government and as an agent of the Guises, in order to induce James to break off his alliance with England in favour of the old alliance with France, and to restore the Roman Church in the country; but the ministers having become informed of his designs, raised such a storm against him that he was driven to make a public renunciation of Popery, and obliged to prosecute his mission by more cautious and circuitous methods than he intended to use. Lennox's evil influence on James in ecclesiastical affairs soon became apparent. On the See of Glasgow becoming vacant, the benefice was appropriated by himself and the title bestowed on Robert Montgomery, minister of Stirling. The Church at once rose up in arms against this flagrant violation of its authority, put Montgomery on his trial for contumacy, found him guilty, and sentenced him to deposition and excommunication. It was at the instance of Melville, who, in this as in many another crisis in the Church's history in his time, was called to the Moderator's chair, that the Assembly took action against Montgomery, and this was done in defiance of a royal inhibition. The inferior courts to which the judicial process at different stages was remitted showed the same determined spirit, so deep and widespread was the indignation that was roused against Lennox by his attempt to thrust bishops anew upon the Church, and against the minister of the Church who had so basely lent himself to it. When the case came before the Presbytery of Glasgow, Montgomery himself appeared, accompanied by the provost and bailies and an escort of soldiers, and produced an interdict under the King's hand against its proceeding. The Presbytery paid no heed to the intruders, and was going on with the business, when the Moderator was ejected from the chair, assaulted, and taken off to prison. Still the Presbytery proceeded till it finished the case and carried out the injunction of the Assembly. Among the crowd gathered at the Presbytery house was a band of students from the University, who in making a demonstration of their sympathy with the ministers were charged by the soldiery, and some blood was shed. The ministers of the East vied with those of the West in supporting the action of the Assembly. John Durie, the most powerful and popular among them, distinguished himself by the boldness with which he spoke against Lennox as the disturber of the peace of the Church. The sentence of excommunication, which had been transmitted to the Edinburgh Presbytery, was pronounced by John Davidson, minister of Liberton, and read in most of the pulpits in Edinburgh and Glasgow on the following Sabbath. A meeting of the Privy Council was immediately called, in which proceedings were taken against the ministers of Edinburgh, and John Durie was banished from the city.

A special meeting of Assembly was called to deal with this serious state of affairs, Melville being still in the chair. In his opening sermon he made a vehement attack on the Court for its renewed attempt to overthrow the Church's order and restore Episcopacy, and spoke of the King's claim to spiritual authority as a 'bludie gullie' thrust into the Commonwealth--a description which the later history of Scotland has sufficiently verified. The House, at one with the Moderator, drew up a statement of the Church's recent grievances, and appointed Melville and some other members to present it to the King at Perth, where he was residing at the time. To Perth accordingly they went. This was a daring step in the circumstances, when there was such exasperation in the Court, and when its councils were led by two such men as Lennox and Arran. 'News was sparpelet athort[7] the cuntry that the ministers war all to be thair massacred.' Melville was warned by a friendly courtier, his namesake Sir James Melville of Halhill, of the risk he ran in carrying out the Assembly's commission. 'I thank God,' he answered, 'I am nocht fleyed nor feible-spirited in the cause and message of Christ. Come what God please to send, our commission sal be dischargit.' When he and the other members of the deputation appeared before the King in Council and read their remonstrance, Arran interfered, when there occurred another of those historic scenes associated with Melville's name, in which he displayed such splendid courage in the resistance of tyranny. An arrogant assailant, like steel striking against flint, always elicited a flash of his noblest manhood. 'Arran began to threttin with thrawin[8] brow and bosting langage. "What," says he, "wha dar subscryve thir treasanable Articles?" "We dar, and will subscryve them,"' answered Melville, taking, as he spoke, the pen from the clerk and putting his name to the document; and then, beckoning to his fellow-deputies, he bade them follow his example, which they all did. The boldness of the deed cowed even Lennox and Arran. They saw that day that 'the Kirk had a bak,' and were glad to dismiss the deputies without further debate.

[Note 7: Spread athwart.]

[Note 8: Frowning.]

The firmness with which the two Court favourites were handled by the ministers inspirited the nobles to execute a plot that had been laid to get the King out of their hands and end their intolerable supremacy. As soon as the King's person had been secured by the Raid of Ruthven, Lennox was banished from the realm, and Arran enjoined to confine himself to his own estate.

For a while the Church had rest and breathed freely after the strain that had been put upon it. A few days after the Raid of Ruthven a great outburst of popular feeling in favour of Presbyterianism took place in Edinburgh, the occasion being the return of John Durie from banishment. 'Ther was a grait concurs of the haill town, wha met him at the Nather Bow; and, going upe the streit, with bear heads and loud voices, sang to the praise of God, and testifeing of grait joy and consolation, the 124th Psalm, "Now Israel may say," etc., till heavin and erthe resoundit. This noyes, when the Duc [of Lennox] being in the town, hard, and ludgit in the Hie-gat, luiked out and saw, he rave his berde for anger, and hasted him af the town.'

The peace of the Church was short-lived. In midsummer of 1583 the King made his escape from the Ruthven lords and betook himself to the Castle of St. Andrews. The old gang at once returned to Court. Lennox had died in exile; but Arran was reinstalled at the Council-board, and immediately renewed the old measures against the ministers, whose part in causing his recent fall made him more than ever determined to crush them. He began with Melville, who was summoned before the Council--it was in February 1584--on a trumped-up charge of using treasonable language in the course of one of his sermons. Melville declined the jurisdiction of the Council on the ground that he was not accused of a civil offence, but of doctrine uttered in the pulpit. His declinature was taken so hotly by the King and Arran that all who were present felt he was as good as a dead man; but 'Mr. Andro, never jarging[9] nor daschit[10] a whit, with magnanimus courage, mightie force of sprit and fouthe[11] of evidence of reason and langage, plainly tauld the King and Council that they presumed ower bauldlie ... to tak upon them to judge the doctrine and controll the ambassadors and messengers of a King and Counsall graiter nor they, and far above tham! "And that," says he, "ye may see weakness, owersight, and rashness in taking upon you that quhilk yie nather aught nor can do" (lowsing a litle Hebrew Byble fra his belt and clanking it down on the burd before King and Chancelar), "thair is," says he, "my instructiones and warrand."' A number of witnesses, well-known enemies of Melville, who had been brought from St. Andrews to support the accusation, gave their evidence, but to no purpose. Instead of being discharged, however, he was condemned for the boldness of his defence--which was construed as a new offence,--and sentenced to imprisonment in the Castle of Edinburgh during his Majesty's pleasure.

[Note 9: Swerving.]

[Note 10: Abashed.]

[Note 11: Abundance.]

Rulers who could so outrage justice as to deprive a subject of his liberty on such a ground were not to be trusted with his life. So all Melville's friends and Melville himself thought. They were persuaded that Arran, at least, was bent on silencing the man who was his most formidable opponent. His friends, quoting the proverb, 'lowes and leiving,'[12] urged him to flight, and he himself resolved on it, having not only his personal safety but also the interests of the Church and the commonweal to consider and safeguard. During the few days he was still left free, he appeared as usual among his friends, and in the best of spirits. At dinner in James Lawson's manse, where many of his friends gathered to meet him, he seemed the only light-hearted man in the company. 'He ate and drank and crakked als merrelie and frie-myndit as at anie tyme and mair,' drinking to his gaoler and fellow-prisoners, and bidding his brethren make ready to follow. While seated at table, the macer of the Council appeared with a warrant charging him to enter the Castle of Blackness within twenty-four hours. When the macer had withdrawn, Melville left the manse, and, confiding his intention to only a few friends, made his escape from the city, accompanied by his brother Roger, and within the twenty-four hours was safely over the Border and lodged in Berwick.

[Note 12: Loose and living.]

Melville's exile at this juncture, when he was so much needed at home to meet the tyranny of the Court, was a severe blow to his brethren in the ministry and to all the friends of the Church. They were entering a heavy battle when they were deprived of their trusted captain. More than James Melville could have said at that time that they felt a 'cauld heavie lumpe' lying on their hearts. The ministers of Edinburgh showed their characteristic spirit in this crisis, and raised such a storm against the King and Council on account of their treatment of Melville that the Court had to defend itself by an apologetic proclamation.

Within a few months after Melville's flight measures were passed through Parliament which upset all that the Church had done during the previous decade to extricate itself from the confusion of the Tulchan Episcopacy. They were devised by Arran and by Archbishop Adamson, who persistently used his influence at Court for the subversion of Presbytery. These measures--'The Black Acts'--declared the supremacy of the King in all matters--ecclesiastical and civil--and made all rejection of his authority a treasonable act: they deprived the Church of the rights of free assembly, free speech, and independent legislation; and they empowered the bishops to reestablish their order in every part of the kingdom. A clause was added requiring all ministers to sign an act of submission to the bishops on penalty of losing their offices and their livings.

On these Acts being proclaimed at the Cross of Edinburgh, the ministers of the city--James Lawson, Walter Balcanquhal, and Robert Pont--appeared and made protest against them, when Arran was so incensed by their conduct that he at once ordered their arrest, and swore he would make Lawson's head 'leap from its halse though it was as big as a haystack.'

More than they were in jeopardy of their lives; every man in the country who had been a pronounced friend of liberty had cause to fear. Lawson, Balcanquhal, and Pont fled, with many others. A warrant had been procured by Archbishop Adamson for the apprehension of James Melville, when he made his escape by open boat to Berwick.

The course of events showed that the ministers had reason for their flight. Some of the most zealous of those left in the country were thrown into prison for refusing to conform to the Acts, or for remembering their banished brethren in public prayer. One minister was tried and sentenced to death on a charge that a letter from one of these brethren had been found in possession of his wife; and though the sentence was not executed, the scaffold was put up, and kept up for some time, before his prison window. Nor were the ministers the only sufferers. Glasgow University, which Melville's teaching and influence had leavened with the principles of liberty, was made to feel the heavy hand of the Government: its professors were imprisoned, its rector was banished, and its gates were closed.

Popular indignation began to break forth in many quarters. In St. Andrews the students went in a body to the Archbishop's palace and warned him that he was courting the fate of Hamilton and Beaton; while visiting Edinburgh, Adamson had to be protected by the police; Montgomery was mobbed at Ayr; and wherever the bishops appeared there were hostile demonstrations on the part of the people.

The Court, however, defied public opinion, and went on with its coercive policy, rigidly enforcing submission to the authority of the bishops. At first the great majority of the ministers refused; but on a clause being added to the deed of submission, to the effect that it required them only to conform 'according to the Word of God,' most of them gave way. The clause was suggested by Adamson, and it reflects his character. It was one of those shrewd devices for causing division among the ministers, and providing a middle way for men distracted by the desire to be faithful to their consciences on the one hand, and the wish to escape persecution on the other, which were often resorted to by the Court throughout the entire course of the struggle against prelacy. Some of the stalwarts of the Church fell into the trap which Adamson had set for them in this shallow compromise, and their example led many others to yield. One of the banished brethren, in a letter written at the time, states that all the ministers in the Lothians and the Merse, with only ten exceptions, had subscribed; that John Erskine of Dun had not only subscribed, but was making himself a pest to the ministers in the North by importuning them to follow his example; that John Craig, so long Knox's colleague, had given in and was speaking hotly against those who held out; that even the redoubtable John Durie had 'cracked his curple'[13] at last; and that the pulpits of Edinburgh were silent, except a very few 'who sigh and sob under the Cross.'

[Note 13: Crupper.]

Events took such a course that the ministers who subscribed might, after all, have held out with a whole skin. They capitulated to their enemies on the very eve of their enemies' fall; for the exasperation of the nation under such insolent tyranny as Arran's could no longer be held in. Davison, the English Ambassador, writing to the Court at this time, says: 'It is incredible how universally the man is hated by all men of all degrees, and what a jealousy is sunken into the heads of some of the wisest here of his ambitious and immoderate thoughts.... His usurp power and disposition of all things, both in Courts, Parliaments, and Sessions, at the appetite of himself and his good lady, with many other things do bewray matter enough to suspect the fruits of ambition and inordinate thirst for rule'; and he adds, 'I find infinite appearances that the young King's course ... doth carry him headlong to his own danger and hazard of his estate. He hath, since the change at St. Andrews, continually followed forth implacable hatred and pursuit against all such as in defence of his life and crown have hazarded their own lives, living, fortunes in all that they have, and now throws himself into the arms of those that have heretofore preferred his mother's satisfaction to his own surety, and do yet aim at that mark, with the apparent danger of religion which hath already received a greater wound by the late confusions and alterations than can be easily repaired.' Other satellites of the Court helped to make the country restive. Adamson especially provoked the people by many petty acts of tyranny, such as the ejection from the manses of the wives of the banished ministers on account of a spirited defence of their husbands, which they had published in reply to charges made against them by the Archbishop.

At the same time the country was visited by two great calamities which were interpreted as divine judgments on the misdeeds of the Government. The harvest was destroyed by heavy rains, and there was an outbreak of the plague of such virulence as to spread terror in all the larger cities. Edinburgh was so desolated, that when James Melville and others of the banished ministers passed through the streets on their return home, they found them empty,--'About alleavin hours he cam rydding in at the watergett of the Abbay, upe throw the Canow-gett, and red in at the Nether Bow, throw the graitt street of Edinbruche to the Wast Port, in all the quhilk way we saw nocht three persons, so that I miskend Edinbruche, and almost forgot that ever I had seen sic a toun.' The people felt that 'the Lord's hand wald nocht stay unto the tyme the Ministers of God and Noble-men war brought hame again.' The banished lords, emboldened by the dissatisfaction of the people and the support of the English Government, and joining with several Border chiefs who had old scores of their own against Arran, invaded the country, marched to Stirling, where the King and Court had retired on hearing of their approach, and took possession of the town. Arran fled, and James was glad to come to terms with the lords.

CHAPTER VI

THE KING'S SURRENDER TO THE CHURCH

'The love of kings is like the blowing of winds
... or the sea which makes
Men hoist their sails in a flattering calm,
And to cut their masts in a rough storm.'

JOHNSON.

This *coup d'etat* left Melville and the other exiled brethren free to return to Scotland, as they did in November 1585. During his stay of nearly two years in England Melville had not been idle. He carried on a correspondence with Protestant ministers in France and Switzerland for the purpose of correcting misrepresentations which Archbishop Adamson had been industriously circulating among them in regard to the conduct of the ministers in Scotland. In all its struggles, from the Reformation to the time of Renwick, the Scottish Church sought to keep the churches of the Continent informed of its affairs and to secure their sympathy. When in London Melville diligently used his influence with leading English statesmen in favour of the cause which he represented. He also took advantage of his proximity to Oxford and Cambridge to visit those Universities, where he was received with the greatest courtesy and respect.

The other ministers who had fled to England had likewise been fully occupied; they had preached in Berwick, in Newcastle, in London, and wherever they found an open door. James Melville had, for a while, most of the banished Ruthven lords in his congregation at Newcastle, and he had sought to invigorate them as the supporters of the liberties of the Church in the event of their returning home to take part again in political life; but, as it proved, with little effect.

The Church soon found that it had gained little by the change of Government. If Arran and his set were its bitter enemies, the new Councillors, the Ruthven lords, were, at the best, indifferent friends. Though they owed their restored power largely to the courageous resistance of the ministers to the Arran administration, and though they had pledged themselves during their exile to use their influence, when opportunity should come, to undo the evils of that administration as they had affected the Church, they were content to secure their own interest and left the Church to look after itself.

Parliament having been summoned to meet in Linlithgow in December 1585, for the purpose of reponing the nobles in their estates and giving its sanction to their administration, the ministers resolved to hold a meeting of Assembly beforehand in Dunfermline to prepare a representation of the Church's interests for the Parliament. When the members of Assembly reached that city they found that the Provost had closed the gates against them, by order, it was said, of the Court. The meeting was held, but adjourned, after resolving that it should be resumed at Linlithgow. James Melville, fresh from his journey from England, arrived in Linlithgow on the eve of the Assembly, and found his brethren much dispirited. They had almost come to a rupture among themselves, high words having passed between those of them who had subscribed the deed of submission to the bishops and those who had refused. This dispute had caused much trouble to Andrew Melville. In a letter of James Melville written at the time to a friend, he says: 'Mr. Andro hath been a traicked[14] man since he cam hame, ryding up and doun all the countrie to see if he might move the brethren to repent and

joyne together.' The Assembly had little hope of Parliament doing
anything towards the repeal of the Black Acts. If the nobles now in
power would not press the King to redress the Church's grievances, it
was certain that he would do nothing in that direction of his own
accord. James was not in a mood to oblige the Church. He could not
conceal his revengeful feelings towards the ministers who had fled with
the Ruthven lords, and especially towards Melville. The Assembly,
however, did its duty. It sent a deputation to the nobles to urge them
to put the Church's claims before the King. The nobles refused, and the
deputation went to the King himself. Melville was its spokesman, and
many sharp and hot words passed between him and James. At length the
King ordered the Assembly to lay before him a statement of its
objections to the Black Acts. This was done, and within twenty-four
hours James issued a reply from his own pen, in which he showed a
conciliatory spirit, and made explanations to take the edge off the
harshness with which the Acts had been framed, but made no alteration in
their substance.

[Note 14: Overtoiled.]

If Parliament did not know when to take occasion by the hand to win
concessions from the King in the interests of liberty, he knew how to
use his opportunity for strengthening his own prerogatives. He brought
forward a measure which the Parliament passed, constituting it a capital
offence to criticise the King's conduct or government, and making it
unlawful for his subjects to enter into any association for political
ends without the consent of the throne.

At this time a fresh *casus belli* between the Church and the Crown
arose through the Church's severe but well-merited handling of
Archbishop Adamson. No man in the kingdom was more responsible for the
recent troubles than Adamson, except Arran, whom he encouraged and
supported in all his arbitrary measures. The minister of the Church who

first opened fire on the Archbishop was James Melville. He had consulted beforehand with his uncle; but those who think he was too amiable to have any fight in him, or that on this or any other occasion he was only doing his uncle's bidding, do not know the man. His courage was as great as his uncle's, if he had a milder manner and a calmer temper; and his action on this occasion was the irrepressible outburst of his honest indignation at Adamson's treachery in the affairs of the Church ever since his elevation to the See of St. Andrews.

In March 1586 the Synod of Fife met at St. Andrews, and James Melville as the retiring Moderator had to preach the opening sermon. It was a full meeting. The Archbishop with a 'grait pontificalite and big countenance' was seated by the preacher's side. The subject of discourse was the evil that had been done to the Church from the time of its planting by the ambitious spirit and corrupt lives of men holding its highest offices. On reaching his application, the preacher, turning to the Archbishop and directing his speech to him personally, recalled his long course of disloyalty to the Church and his persistent efforts to overthrow its discipline, as well as all the injuries he had done to religion by his avarice and ambition: he spoke of him as a dangerous member who needed to be courageously cut off in order to save the body; and then, addressing himself to the Assembly, exhorted it to 'play the chirurgeon!' This bold and unexpected attack unmanned the Archbishop--'he was sa dashit and strucken with terror and trembling that he could skarse sitt, to let be stand on his feet.' It was manifest that the Moderator had the whole House at his back, and it at once entered on a process against Adamson. At first he declined its jurisdiction, boasting that it was rather his place to judge the Assembly. At length, however, he condescended to defend himself; and the process ended in his excommunication. A day or two after he retaliated by excommunicating, on his own authority, within his own church, Andrew Melville and other brethren. He also despatched to the King an appeal against the Synod's sentence, defying the sentence at the same time by appearing in his own pulpit on the following Sabbath. On the same Sabbath Melville was preaching in his own college chapel to a crowded congregation; and a neighbouring laird, with a number of his friends, having come to the city on that Sabbath to hear Melville, there was an unusual stir which drew most of the townsfolk to the chapel. When the last bell was ringing, and Adamson was about to enter the pulpit, a *canard* reached him to the effect that a body of local gentry and the citizens gathered within the college gates had formed a conspiracy to seize him and hang him on the spot. Calling to his servants to guard him, he ran out of the church and sought refuge in the steeple, and it took the magistrates all their skill to persuade him to leave his hiding-place and accept their convoy to the palace--'he was halff against his will ruggit[15] out, and halff borne and careit away' amid the derision of the onlookers.

[Note 15: Pulled.]

Adamson had appealed to the Assembly which was to meet in May. The King, being indignant at the treatment the Archbishop had received, was resolved to get the sentence annulled, and he set himself to tune the Assembly to his mind. He called a meeting by royal proclamation, and gave it out that he would attend it himself. The temper of the Assembly was such that the resolutions that were to effect the King's object had to be cautiously framed, and were carried by a bare majority of votes. The Court, without judging the Synod's proceedings and sentence, and only after Adamson had made an apology for his pretentions to authority in the Church, and had given a promise to drop them for the future, resolved to restore him. The case had been no sooner disposed of than Melville was summoned before the King and commanded to go into ward north of the Tay, that the Archbishop might have a better chance of recovering his lost prestige--a restriction which, however, was soon removed on a strong representation being made to the King of the loss which the University was suffering by the banishment of Melville.

From this time the Archbishop fell into disgrace, both for his shameful
public career and for the offences of his private life, especially his
extravagance and consequent debts. Two years later he was deposed by the
Assembly, when the King cast him off, and gave the temporalities of his
see to one of the Court favourites. After that Adamson never lifted his
head. When he had fallen into poverty and sickness he made a pitiful
appeal to Melville, which was most generously met. His old opponent
visited him, and for months provided for him out of his own purse; and
it was through the good offices of both the Melvilles that he was able
to make his peace with the Church before he died. Perhaps it is this
last act of humbleness, when he had lost all repute with the world,
that gives him his best claim on our respect.

For some months previous to the Assembly in which Adamson's case was
disposed of, the King had been exerting himself so to manage the members
amenable to his influence, that he should not only secure his object in
this particular business, but at the same time prevail with the Assembly
to take a step backward in its general polity. He dared not propose much
more than titular precedence for the bishops--a concession only wrung
from the Assembly; and for a ***quid pro quo*** he had to give his consent
to a measure for carrying out the provisions of the Second Book of
Discipline by organising presbyteries and synods throughout the country.
This was of course another compromise, but the Church's concessions were
reduced to a minimum. James could only secure a footing for the bishops,
and bide his time for restoring their supremacy.

In the Parliament of 1587, when Melville was present as a commissioner
from the Assembly, a measure was passed, which, though it originated
with the Court and was not so intended, dealt a serious blow to the
hopes of the promoters of Episcopacy. The King had just attained his
twenty-first year, and there was a law in the statute-book providing
that all heirs of estates which had been forfeited through any cause

should, on reaching their majority, have the opportunity of reclaiming them. Advantage was taken of this law to revoke grants of Crown lands made during the King's minority; and all the Church lands were annexed to the Crown. This measure stripped the bishops of their benefices and abolished their legal status, and so cancelled the chief ground on which the Court had contended for the maintenance of their order. By this measure the King, in his need or greed, or both, played for once into the hands of the Church.

In the following year, 1588, the prodigious attempt of Philip to invade England and overthrow the Protestant power in the two kingdoms very greatly strengthened the Presbyterian cause in Scotland, and made Episcopacy more than ever repugnant to the people, as having in it so much of the leaven of the Old Church. Whatever roused the Protestant spirit of the country gave Presbytery a firmer hold as the Church system most antagonistic to Popery, and also to arbitrary government which seeks in Popery its natural ally. At every crisis such as that which now arose, it made a fresh appeal to the deepest feelings of the nation.

At the time when the Armada was approaching our shores the country had no confidence in the patriotism of the King. There were sinister suspicions of his attitude to Romanism, caused by the favours shown at Court to nobles of that faith; by his retention of many of its adherents in his service, and his reluctance to take action against the Romish priests, the Jesuits, and the rest of the army of Papal emissaries who were sowing treason throughout the land. All through his life James was characterised by a singular unseasonableness in his activity. 'There is a time,' says the preacher, 'to every purpose under the heaven,' but with James there was always an incongruity between the time and the purpose. The year before, he had scandalised the Court by dancing and giggling at a levee held immediately after his mother's death; and now, when he should have been arming the country against the Spanish invasion, he was engaged in writing an academic treatise against the

Pope. Perhaps his conduct was due to a deeper fault in his character--his ingrained duplicity. As, after his accession to the English throne, he sought to thwart the anti-Papal policy of his own Government when Spain was threatening the Protestant power in Germany, so now he may have been dissembling his real sympathies in writing against the Papacy. At all events, he never showed by any act of his reign that he dreaded the Papal power as much as he dreaded that of the Scottish Presbyterians or the English Puritans.

The Armada brought Melville once more to the front. It was his voice that roused the nation to a sense of its danger, and his energy that organised the nation to meet it. He summoned the Assembly, being Moderator at the time: the Assembly stirred up the nobles and the burgesses, and the whole nation joined to offer resistance to the invasion.

From this time the favourable tide for the fortunes of Presbytery which had set in previous to the Armada flowed with a rush, which within a few years carried it to undisputed ascendency in the land. The people's attachment to it was too strong for James, and even within his own Council it had come to be recognised that acquiescence in it was inevitable. Maitland, Lethington's brother, the Chancellor of the kingdom, who was the strongest man in the Council, and for long a supporter of the King's policy in ecclesiastical affairs, was now won over, by the logic of events, to its support. He had the sense to perceive that the kingdom could never prosper till the Church was satisfied, and that the Church could never be satisfied with any other than its own freely chosen economy. He also saw that if the King was to maintain friendship with the English Government, he must sever himself from those forces in the country that were opposed to the Church, as they were all under the suspicion of working in the interests of the power which had made so determined an attempt at the overthrow of the neighbouring kingdom. 'He helde the King upon twa groundes sure, nather to cast out with the Kirk nor with England.' Prelacy, he knew, was but the King's choice for the nation: Presbytery was the nation's choice for itself. Maitland's influence was great with the King, and from this time it was used steadily in favour of a new departure in his Church policy.

At the same time there arose, in the person of Robert Bruce, minister of Edinburgh, one who rendered powerful service to the Presbyterian cause, and who, in the whole history of the struggle, was singular in this respect, that while possessing the entire confidence of his brethren he also carried great weight in the Council of the King. Of good family, second son of the Laird of Airth, he had studied for the Bar and then abandoned it for the Church. For many years of his life he had been conscious of striving against the work of grace in his heart, and against the conviction that he ought to devote himself to the ministry, and had thereby suffered sore trouble of conscience. At last a crisis came, which he describes as 'a court of justice holden on his soul,' which 'chased' him to his grace. Immediately thereafter he sought the counsel of Melville, to whom he had been greatly attracted, who encouraged him to enter the ministry, and under whom he was trained for it. Bruce commanded respect from all classes and on all hands; 'the godlie for his puissant and maist moving doctrine lovit him; the wardlings for his parentage and place reverenced him; and the enemies for bath stude in awe of him.' Bruce was a special friend of Chancellor Maitland, through whom he was received with favour at the Court; and he brought Maitland and Melville together and made them friends.

His marriage, which took place in 1589, was used by James as an occasion for a public demonstration of his reconciliation to the Church. Before leaving for Denmark to fetch his bride, he made Bruce an extraordinary member of his Council, professing at the same time such confidence in him as he might have given to a viceroy, which indeed Bruce virtually became. During the King's absence the nation enjoyed a tranquillity unknown before in his reign, chiefly due to the influence of Bruce and his brethren. James Melville had good ground for what he said at the Assembly in August 1590: 'We, and the graittest and best number of our flockes, halff bein, ar, and mon be his [the King's] best subjects, his strynthe, his honour. A guid minister (I speak it nocht arrogantlie, but according to the treuthe!) may do him mair guid service in a houre nor manie of his sacrilegious courteours in a yeir.' At the Queen's coronation the ministers took the chief part in the ceremony. It was Bruce who anointed her, and, with David Lindsay, minister of Leith, placed the crown on her head. Melville was chosen by the King to prepare and recite the Stephaniskion, as the coronation ode was called, and the King was so pleased with it that he gave him effusive thanks. On the following Sabbath James was present in St. Giles', and in the presence of the congregation acknowledged the services rendered by Bruce and the ministers to the country and the crown during his absence, and promised to turn a new leaf in the government of the kingdom. He was also present at the next General Assembly, when he broke forth in such fervent laudation of the Church that he might have made the oldest and staunchest adherents of Presbytery reproach themselves for the coldness of their own attachment to it: 'He fell furth in praising God, that he was borne in suche a tyme as the tyme of the light of the Gospell, to suche a place as to be king in suche a Kirk, the sincerest Kirk in the world. "The Kirk of Geneva," said he, "keepeth Pasche and Yule; what have they for them?--they have no institutioun. As for our nighbour Kirk in England, it is an evill said masse in English, wanting nothing but the liftings.[16] I charge you, my good people, ministers, doctors, elders, nobles, gentlemen, and barons, to stand to your puritie, and to exhort the people to doe the same; and I forsuith, so long as I bruike my life and crowne, sall mainteane the same against all deidlie," etc. The Assemblie so rejoiced, that there was nothing but loud praising of God, and praying for the King for a quarter of an houre.'[17]

[Note 16: Raising of the Host.]

[Note 17: Calderwood's *History*, v. 109.]

The *entente cordiale* between the King and the ministers was not of
long duration. His promises of amended government were soon forgotten;
the lawlessness of the nobles continued unchecked; agents of Rome were
again busy in the country in collusion with the Popish nobles, and
nothing was done to counteract them. In these circumstances the
ministers could not keep silence, and none of them spoke more strongly
against the laxity of the Government than Robert Bruce, the man the King
had so recently and so specially honoured, who reproached James with the
fact that during his absence in Denmark more reverence was paid to his
shadow than had been shown since his return to his person. The outrages
perpetrated by the King's illegitimate cousin, the madcap Bothwell, were
largely laid to James's door, as the doings of a spoiled favourite of
the Court: and the unpunished murder of the popular Earl of Moray, the
'Bonnie Earl,' by Huntly--one of the worst crimes even of that
lawless time, and of complicity in which the King himself was
suspected--aggravated the discontent of the nation.

It was at such a time of disorder and irritation in the country that the
measure was passed by Parliament--the Act of 1592--by which all
previous legislation in favour of Episcopacy was swept off the
statute-book and the Church re-established on the basis of the Second
Book of Discipline. Had this Act been passed two years earlier, it might
have been ascribed to the goodwill of the King; but in the circumstances
in which it was brought forward, it was regarded as a piece of policy,
adopted on the recommendation of the Chancellor for the purpose of
recovering for the King the popularity he had lost during that interval,
by the causes we have mentioned.

CHAPTER VII

THE POPISH LORDS--MELVILLE AND THE KING AT FALKLAND PALACE

'The king he movit his bonnet to him,
He ween'd he was a king as weel as he.'

Johnie Armstrong.

The end of the Church's troubles in Scotland was still far off. No sooner had the constitution of 1592, which promised to secure her peace and liberty, been set down in the statute-book, than the forces of reaction, headed by the Crown, began to work for the undoing of it; and the Church was to pass through a century of almost continuous struggle and of many and bitter disappointments--a century which had great part in the making of Scotland--before that constitution was finally ratified.

The slackness of James towards the Popish agents, who had resumed their intrigues in the country, has been referred to. Those best informed in public affairs both in England and Scotland shared the indignation and alarm in the matter which were expressed by the ministers. One day, in the very year after the Armada, as James was in the Tolbooth with the Lords of Session, a packet was put into his hands from the English Queen containing intercepted treasonable letters from the Popish lords in Scotland to the King of Spain and the Duke of Parma, and accompanied by the following letter in Elizabeth's own hand, in which she rates him for his fatuous lenity towards subjects who had joined hands with the enemies of his kingdom:--

'MY DEERE BROTHER,--I have ere now assured you, that als long
as I found you constant in amitie towards me, I would be your
faithfull watche, to shunne all mishappes or dangers that, by
assured intelligence, I might compasse to give you. And
according to my good devotioun and affectioun, it hath pleased
God to make me, of late, so fortunat as to have intercepted a
messinger (whom I keepe safe for you), that carried letters of
high treasoun to your persone and kingdome; and can doe no
lesse, than with most gladenesse, send you the discovered
treasoun, suche as you may see, as in a glasse, the true
portrature of my late wairning letters; which, if then it had
pleased you follow, als weill as read, you might have taiken
their persons, receaved their treasoun, and shunned their
further strenthening, which hath growne daylie by your too
great neglecting and suffering of so manie practises which, at
the beginning, might easilie have been prevented.

'Permitt me, I pray you, my deere brother, to use als muche
plainnesse as I beare you sinceritie, your supposing to deale
moderatlie and indifferentlie to both factions, and not to take
nor punishe, at the first, so notorious offenders, as suche as
durst send to a forrane king for forces to land in your land
under what pretence soever, without your special directioun,
the same never punished; but rather, holde foote deere and
neere, with a parentage of neare allya. Good Lord! me thinke I
doe but dreame: no king a weeke would beare this! Their forces
assembled, and held neere your persoun, held plotts to take
your persoun neere the seaside; and that all this wrapped up
with giving them offices, that they mighte the better
accomplishe their treasoun! These be not the formes of
governments that my yeeres have experimented: I would yours had

noucht, for I sweare unto you myne sould never in like sort.

'I exhort you be not subject to such weaknesse, as to suffer
such lewdnesse so long to roote, as all your strenth sall not
plucke up (which God forbid!), which to shunne, after you have
perused this great packet that I sent you, take speedie order
lest you linger too long; and take counsell of few, but of wise
and trustie. For if they suspect your knowledge they will
shunne your apprehensioun. Therefore of a suddantie they must
be clapped up in safer custodie than some others have been,
which hath bred their laughter. You see my follie when I am
entered to matter that toucheth you so neere. I know not how to
ende but with my prayers to God to guide you for your best. My
agent with you sall tell you the rest.

'Your most aproved loving sister and consignesse,

　　　　'ELIZABETH R.'[18]

[Note 18: Calderwood's *History*, v. 9.]

An incident which occurred at the close of 1592, and which is known in
our history as 'The Spanish Blanks,' brought to an acute crisis the
suspicion and discontent of the country, and especially of the
ministers. A Papist of the name of Kerr was about to embark on his ship,
which was lying off Fairlie Roads on the Ayrshire coast, when he was
arrested by a posse of Glasgow students and local gentry, with Knox the
minister of Paisley at their head. In conversation with some of the
people, Kerr had led them to suspect that he was bound for Spain as the
agent of some plot, and information to this effect was immediately
communicated to the authorities in the neighbourhood, and among others
to Knox. Only a month before, at the instance of Melville, the ministers
had formed a vigilance committee to gather reports from every parish in

the country of any sinister movements on the part of the Papists, and to lay these before the Council, that steps might be taken at once to defeat them. Kerr's apprehension was a proof of the efficiency of this organisation. A search having been made, there were found in his possession, along with many treasonable letters, several sheets of paper containing no writing. They were addressed to the King of Spain, however, and bore the signatures and seals of the three chief Popish lords--Huntly, Angus, and Errol. Attached to these documents was a commission to a Jesuit named Crichton, to fill up the blanks, and in such a way--so it transpired afterwards--as to invite Philip to invade the country, and to pledge to him the support of these nobles. Kerr and an accomplice, Graham of Fintry, were brought before the Council and confessed the plot; and a few days after the arrest of Kerr, before the report of it had spread through the country, the Earl of Angus, having occasion to come to Edinburgh, was seized by the magistrates and confined in the Castle.

The King was absent from the city at the time attending the marriage festivities of the Earl of Mar, and an urgent request was sent to him by the ministers of Edinburgh and his own Council to return and take steps to bring the conspirators to justice. James, instead of thanking the ministers and councillors for their diligence in the matter, blamed them for their super-serviceableness, and so gave the impression that he was in sympathy with the plot. Kerr himself, in a letter to the King, went the length of saying that he and his friends had no doubt that they would have his countenance in their enterprise; and Calderwood says:--'It appeareth the chief conspirators have had his [the King's] expresse or tacite consent, or at least have perceaved him inclyned that way, whereupon they have presumed.' Events confirmed the suspicion, if it wanted confirmation, of James's secret leanings to the party that had been guilty of treason. Only one of them--Graham, the most insignificant of their number--paid the penalty of his crime; Kerr and the Earl of Angus escaped from prison with the connivance of the authorities;

Huntly, who had been summoned to stand trial before the Privy Council, retired to his own territory and defied the Government, and it was only when he could no longer resist the popular will that the King took action against him. At the head of a considerable force, James set out to seize him; but when the army reached Aberdeen it was found that the Earl had retired further north to the Caithness moors. The subsequent treatment of the rebel lords showed that the King had no heart in their prosecution--indeed, in an unguarded moment, while conversing with one of the few nobles who were reckoned friends of the Protestant cause, Lord Hamilton, he let out this fact. Had it not been for the pressure of the ministers, nothing would have been done. James trifled with the business: he scolded and coaxed the ministers in turn; he threatened them, and then gave way and promised to bring the offenders to trial, but still made no move; he allowed the conspirators to appear in public and to have interviews with himself in which he made it apparent that they had little to fear at his hands; he tampered with his own law officers in the traitors' interest; and through his influence with Parliament they were virtually absolved and their forfeitures cancelled. But the ministers were stronger and far more really representative of the nation than the Parliament--a fact which markedly characterises this long crucial period of Scottish history, and which must always be borne in mind for a right understanding of events.

The two Melvilles took the lead in the Church's action. At the Synod of Fife, September 1593, excommunication was pronounced on the Popish lords; and steps were taken to hold an early meeting in Edinburgh of commissioners from the counties to adopt such measures as would secure the ends of justice. At this convention, delegates were appointed to meet with the King and represent to him the necessity of taking vigorous action against the lords. The interview took place at Jedburgh, where the King had gone to repress some Border tumult. 'We war bot bauchlie[19] lukit upon,' says James Melville, who was one of the delegates.--'Our Assembly of Fife was bitterly inveyit against, namlie my uncle Mr. Andro and Mr. David Black.' Before the interview closed, the King became more gracious, and he dismissed the delegates with fair promises; but his real answer was the subsequent passing through Parliament of an Act of Oblivion in favour of the lords, which he urged on the unkingly ground that, if severe measures were taken against them, they would go 'to armes and get forean assistance quhilk might wrack King, Country, and Relligion.'

[Note 19: Sorrily.]

Parliament had given way to the King: but the ministers kept their ground. The Assembly of May 1594 ratified the deed of the Synod of Fife in excommunicating the Popish lords, and appointed another commission to meet with the King and urge him in the matter, James Melville being again one of the delegates and their spokesman. The manner in which the King received them was very different from that in which he had received the deputation at Jedburgh, and surprised them by its friendliness. He expressed his regret at the misunderstandings that had arisen between himself and the Church, heard the statements of the delegates with apparent favour, and promised to summon Parliament for the earliest convenient day to take measures for the punishment of the excommunicated lords. At the close of the conference the King detained James Melville for a private interview, and sent through him a friendly message to his uncle, acknowledging both to be most faithful and trusty subjects. From this time, for the space of two years, James Melville by the King's command went a great deal about the Court. 'Courting' did not go with his heart, but he was reconciled to it by the hope that he might be of service in bringing the King into better relations with the Church. The King's motive in inviting him to Court may be inferred from an incident which occurred one day when he had been conferring with the King on Church affairs. As Melville left the room the King was overheard saying to a courtier, 'I have streaked his mouth with cream.' James little knew the man, than whom there was not among his subjects one less likely to be seduced from his convictions by a king's flattery or favours. When the King found after a two years' trial that he was untamable, James Melville's 'Courting' days ceased.

The King's change of policy in the business concerned and his adoption of a more conciliatory attitude to the ministers are not difficult to explain. He had come to realise that they were too strong for him: they had the country with them, while towards himself there was a universal feeling of suspicion and discontent. Moreover, the ministers had a strong ally in Queen Elizabeth, who continued to make angry remonstrances with James on his treatment of the rebel lords. In one stinging letter she said 'she could only pray for him, and leave him to himself. She did not know whether sorrow or shame had the upper hand, when she had learned that he had let those escape against whom he had such evident proof. Lord! what wonder grew in her that he should correct them with benefits and simply banished them to those they loved. She more than smiled to read their childish, foolish, witless excuses, turning their treasons' bills to artificers' reckonings, one billet lacking only, item, so much for the cord they best merited.'[20]

[Note 20: Cunningham's *History*, i. 424.]

James dared not longer defy the feeling of the country, and accordingly Parliament was summoned in June 1594 and the trial of the Popish lords proceeded with, the King professing the greatest zeal in it, and declaring that, as he had found 'plaister and medicine' unavailing in dealing with the traitors, he would now 'use fire as the last remedie.' It fell to Parliament to choose those who composed the court in trials for treason--the Lords of the Articles they were called,--and some of those who were chosen on this occasion were notoriously tainted with treason themselves. Melville, who was present in the Parliament as a commissioner of the Church, attended the opening of the court, and, addressing the King and the judges, admonished them to deal with the

cause as the laws of the realm and the safety of the country required.
'It is true,' he said, 'manie thinke it a mater of great weight to
overthrow the estate of three so great men. I grant it is so: yitt it is
a greater mater to overthrow and expell out of this countrie three farre
greater; to witt, true religioun, the quietnesse of the commoun weale,
and the King's prosperous estat.' He then challenged the composition of
the court: '"There come some heere to reasoun who have no interest, but
ought to be excluded by all law,"--meaning of the Pryour of Pluscardie,
brother to the Lord Setoun, who was after made chanceller. Some
answered, that he was a man of honorable place, President of the
Sessioun. Mr. Andrew answered, more honorable were debarred from place
among the Lords of the Articles. The King confessed it was true, and
promised it sould be amended. "Nixt," said Mr. Andrew, "there are some
on the Articles justlie suspected partiall, and almost als guiltie as
the persons that are to be tryed." The Abbot of Inchaffrey and Mr.
Edward Bruce sitting together laughed. The King asked at Mr. Andrew who
it was that was suspected? Mr. Andrew said, "One laughing there." Mr.
Edward asked if he meant of him. Mr. Andrew answered, "If yee confesse
your self guiltie, I will not purge you: but I meant of Inchaffrey
there, beside you." The King sayeth to Mr. Edward, "That is Judas'
questioun, 'Is it I, Maister?'"--whereat was muche laughter.'

The forfeiture of the lords was agreed to, all but unanimously. But it
was easier to pronounce this sentence than to execute it. Huntly, the
chief traitor, defied the Government from his stronghold in the North,
where he was all-powerful. The Crown had no standing army, and depended
in military undertakings on the great feudal lords, one of the greatest
of whom, Argyle, the potentate of the West Highlands, was ready to take
the field against his rival, Huntly, in the North. He invaded the
Gordon district with a strong force, but was beaten by Huntly at
Glenlivet. The Crown then raised an army of its own, by proclamation,
and the King marched north with the force, accompanied on his own
command by the two Melvilles, that their presence might be a pledge to

the country of his sincerity and zeal in the business. On the army
reaching Aberdeen, it was found that Huntly and his friends had again
fled to Caithness, and it was resolved to go on to the district of the
rebels and demolish their strongholds. The weather was so severe,
however, that the army could not move out of Aberdeen for a whole month;
and by that time all the money the King had in hand for the expense of
the war was exhausted, and it became necessary to raise more. The means
he took to do this showed his estimate of the ministers' hold on the
country. He sent James Melville south to enlist their services in
procuring the money, and with him a letter in his own hand to the
ministers of Edinburgh, whom he addressed as his 'trusty friends,' in
which he made a fervent appeal to them to rouse the burgesses to do
their duty in the matter, and declared that, rather than that there
should be any miscarriage of justice, he would 'give crown, life, and
all else God had put into his hands.'

The King's message had been no sooner despatched than a difference of
opinion arose among his advisers as to the course to be pursued with the
rebels. A majority was in favour of taking no further action, while
Melville vehemently urged that the army should advance into Huntly's
territory and overthrow his chief stronghold, the castle of Strathbogie.
The King could better afford to differ from the Council than from
Melville, whose advice he adopted and at once put into execution; and
when the rebels heard of the destruction of Strathbogie, they believed
that at last the King was serious in the business, and Huntly and his
friends fled from the country in despair.

This expedition took place in the fall of 1594. Before another year was
over the King's attitude towards the Church was again hostile, or
rather, his latent hostility began to be again evident and active. The
removal from the Court of the Chancellor about this time, through an
illness of which he soon died, so far accounts for the King's relapse in
his relations with the ministers, as for some time Maitland's influence

had been used in encouraging him to cultivate their friendship.

In 1595, the King incurred one of those periodic explosions of
Melville's indignation, which were provoked by his own incurable
distrust of the ministers, and his persistent effort to deprive them of
liberty of speech in the pulpit. Mr. David Black of St. Andrews, one of
the most zealous and honoured ministers of the Church, had made an enemy
of Balfour of Burley, who has already been referred to in connection
with outrages on citizens of St. Andrews. In revenge, Balfour raised
calumnious charges against Black of disloyal utterances in the pulpit,
and got them conveyed, through acquaintances among the courtiers, to the
King's ears; Melville, as his friend, and as having been the means of
bringing him to the city, being also reported to the King as involved in
his offences. The two were summoned to appear before the King and
Council at Falkland to answer the accusations that had been made against
them. While Black and his accusers were being heard, Melville, who had
not been called, and who was determined that he would see justice done
to his friend, knocking at the door, burst into the Council Chamber,
'and efter humble reverence done to the King, he braks out with grait
libertie of speitche, letting the King planlie to knaw, that quhilk
dyvers tymes befor, with small lyking, he haid tooned in his ear, "Thait
thair was twa Kings in Scotland, twa Kingdomes, and twa Jurisdictiones:
Thir was Chryst Jesus, etc.: And gif the King of Scotland, civill King
James the Saxt, haid anie judicator or cause thair, presentlie, it sould
nocht be to judge the fathfull messanger of Jesus Chryst, the King,
etc., bot (turning him to the Lard of Burley, standing there) this
trator, wha hes committed divers poinets of his treasone against his
Majestie's civill lawes, to his grait dishonour and offence of his guid
subjects, namlie, taking of his peacable subjects on the night out of
thair housses, ravishing of weimen, and receating within his hous of the
King's rebels and forfault enemies!"

'With this, Burley falles down on his knees to the King, and craves

justice. "Justice!" sayes Mr. Andro, "wald to God yow haid it! Yow wald nocht be heir to bring a judgment from Chryst upon the King, and thus falslie and unjustlie to vex and accuse the fathfull servants of God!"
The King began, with sum countenances and speitches, to command silence and dashe him; bot he, insurging with graitter bauldnes and force of langage, buir out the mater sa, that the King was fean to tak it upe betwix tham with gentill termes and mirrie talk; saying, "They war bathe litle men, and thair hart was at thair mouthe!'" Melville's boldness stopped the proceedings, and there and then the trial took end.

We have now reached a period, 1596, just midway between the Reformation and the Covenant, when the Crown resumed its openly hostile policy towards the Church, laying upon her once more the heavy hand of oppression. From this date it pursued its object--the introduction of Episcopacy--more energetically than before. For the first decade of the renewed struggle it was strenuously opposed by the leaders of the Assembly; but thereafter, when the leaders had been silenced or banished, there was a free course for tyranny, and during the next fifty years the fortunes of the Church suffered an eclipse. To see the emergence we have to look ahead to 1632-1638, the period of the Covenant and the Glasgow Assembly, when there came that revival of the spirit of the Church which prepared her for her ultimate conflict and hard-won victory in 1688.

The cloud, no bigger than a man's hand, had already appeared on the horizon in the changed attitude of the King, which we have just noted; but there was no one able to foresee the storm it portended, which was to rage so long and so cruelly before the sky cleared again.

James Melville speaks of 1596 as to be 'markitt for a special perriodic and fatall yeir to the Kirk of Scotland,' and he enters on his narrative of it 'with a sorrowful heart and drouping eyes,' so 'doolful' was the decay it ushered in. The declension is not to be wondered at; for where has a Church been found in which such prolonged oppression as the Scottish Church had been subjected to, did not weary the patience and damp the zeal of all but the most resolved members of its Communion? Had we been present at one of the diets of the Assembly, held in March of this 'fatall' year, we should have witnessed a scene which might have been taken as an augury of good to the Church, rather than of evil. It was a day set apart for humiliation and the renewal of the Covenant, and no day had been seen like it, since the Reformation, in the spiritual fervour which was evoked. The exhortations of the preacher drew forth such sighs and sobs and weeping, that the House was turned into a Bochim; and when those present were asked to signify their entrance into a new covenant with God, the congregation rose *en masse* and held up their hands. Similar scenes took place in the Synods and Presbyteries to which the movement extended. 'I am certaine,' says James Melville, 'by the experience found in my selff and maney others present in these meittinges, that the Assemblies of the saintes in Scotland wes nevir more beautiful and gloriouse by the manifold and mightie graces of the presence of the Holy Spirit.'

This devotional diet of the Assembly was held as the prelude to a work of reformation in religion and morals on which the Church had set its heart, and which, beginning with the ministry, was to be sought also in the Parliament, in the Court, in the seats of justice, in every household, in all ranks and classes, from the King to the meanest of his subjects, to those who were in the highways and hedges, to the 'pypers, fidlers, songsters, sorners, peasants, and beggars.' It was an exhaustive programme; and the ministers gave undeniable proofs of their sincerity by setting themselves to put their own house in order, and drawing up ordinances for sifting their own ranks and 'rypping' out their own ways. The scheme, as it applied to others, was too much of the nature of a magisterial inquisition for sin to do credit to its promoters' wisdom, if the ends they sought did honour to their hearts. No doubt, the condition of the country was such as to distress every good citizen and to make any remedy welcome. There was clamant need for reform in every department of the State. The administration of justice was, by its corruption and its ineffectiveness in the punishment of crime, a disgrace to the country. These were matters of public scandal, calling clearly for public agitation and reform; but in matters of private and domestic life the ministers should have been content with exhortation and example as their means of reformation. A moral police proved then as intolerable and ineffectual as it must always be. Our concern is to vindicate, not the absolute wisdom of Melville and the other ministers of that day, but their thoroughgoing and disinterested zeal for the purity and godliness of their nation, of which this scheme of reform is a signal proof.

The movement of the Assembly was soon checked by fresh troubles in the State. It was well known that Philip had never ceased to chafe at the humiliation inflicted on him by the disastrous end of the Armada, and that he was burning for revenge. In January of this year James had issued a Proclamation in which he declared that the ambition of the King of Spain to make conquest of the Crown and Kingdom of England was manifest to all who had the least 'spunk of understanding'; that to have such a neighbour settled on the borders of Scotland would be attended with the eminent hazard of civil and spiritual thraldom; and that it was therefore necessary to unite all their force and concur with England in the defence of their ancient liberties and in preserving the isle from the tyranny of strangers. At the Assembly last held the King had been present, and had urged that contributions should be made from the whole realm for this purpose, when Melville rose and told him, with his usual plainness of speech, that if the estates of the Popish lords were applied, as they should be, to the defence of the country, no contributions would be needed from the people.

We can imagine the shock of alarm with which in these circumstances the nation heard that the Earl of Huntly and his associates had returned to

Scotland, and the rising exasperation as it became evident that the King was disposed to let them settle down peaceably. Who could fathom the mind or trust the intentions of a King who roused the nation to resist Philip, while he at the same time harboured the faction that was prepared, when Philip appeared, to give him welcome?

A change had recently taken place in the ***personnel*** of the Government that did not tend to allay the apprehensions which the return of the rebel lords awakened in the country. A Commission of eight had been appointed to manage the King's private property and the Crown estates; but though nominally only a Finance Committee, 'the Octavians,' as they were called, soon got the reins of government into their hands; and of this new Cabinet, 'one-half ... war suspecte Papists, and the rest little better.'

In August 1596 the Estates were summoned to meet in Falkland and consult what was to be done with the Popish lords. From the manner in which the meeting was called, it was evident that the King and his ministers had resolved to condone the crimes of Huntly and his allies, and to restore them to their honours and estates. The summons was confined to those members who were friendly to the lords, and to such of the ministers of the Church as might be expected to yield to the wishes of the Court. Melville, however, appeared with a commission from the Church which gave him authority to watch over its interests on all occasions on which they might be in danger. When the King, before the sitting had begun, demanded the reason of his presence, and bade him go home, Melville answered that he must first discharge the commission intrusted to him by God and the Church. The session having opened, the King ordered that the members should take their seats as their names were called from the list. Melville, without his name being called, was among the first to enter, when the King's challenge gave him the opportunity he sought of delivering his soul: 'Sir, I have a calling to com heir be Chryst Jesus the King, and his Kirk, wha hes speciall entres in this tourn,[21] and against quhilks directlie this Conventioun is mett; charging yow and your Esteattes in his nam, and of his Kirk, that yie favour nocht his enemies whom he hattes, nor go nocht about to call hame and mak citiciners, these that has traterouslie sought to betrey thair citie and native countrey to the crewall Spainyard, with the overthrow of Chryst's Kingdome, fra the quhilk they have bein thairfor maist justlie cutt of as rotten members; certifeing, if they sould do in the contrair, they sould feill the dint of the wrathe of that King and his Esteattes!' On the King interrupting him and commanding him to go out, Melville obeyed, thanking God that 'they haid knawin his mynd and gottin his message dischargit.'

[Note 21: Interest in this business.]

The business at this meeting of the Estates was all 'chewed meit.' The Resolutions were prepared by the King for a House packed with his nominees, and it was agreed to license the return of the lords and to receive their submission.

In September the Commission of Assembly met at Cupar and appointed a deputation, consisting of the two Melvilles and other two ministers, to lay before the King their complaint regarding the decision of the Parliament, and to crave him to prevent it being carried into effect. The interview between Andrew Melville, the spokesman of the deputation, and King James at Falkland Palace is an event of which the memory will live in Scotland as long as it is a nation, and which ranks in moral dignity and dramatic interest with the greatest scenes in history. When did a subject ever use a manlier freedom with his Sovereign? When did mere titular kingship more plainly shrink into insignificance in presence of the moral majesty vested in the spirit of a true man? No writer can afford to describe the scene in other words than those of James Melville:--

'Mr. Andro Melvill, Patrik Galloway, James Nicolsone, and I, cam to Falkland, whar we fand the King verie quyet. The rest leyed upon me to be speaker, alleaging I could propone the mater substantiuslie, and in a myld and smothe maner, quhilk the King lyked best of. And, entering in the Cabinet with the King alan, I schew his Majestie, That the Commissionars of the Generall Assemblie, with certean uther breithring ordeanit to watche for the weill of the Kirk in sa dangerous a tym, haid convenit at Cowper. At the quhilk word the King interrupts me and crabbotlie quarrels our meitting, alleaging it was without warrand and seditius, making our selves and the countrey to conceave feir whar was na cause. To the quhilk, I beginning to reply, in my maner, Mr. Andro doucht nocht abyd it, bot brak af upon the King in sa zealus, powerfull, and unresistable a maner, that whowbeit the King used his authoritie in maist crabbit and colerik maner, yit Mr. Andro bure him down, and outtered the Commission as from the mightie God, calling the King bot "God's sillie vassall"; and, taking him be the sleive, sayes this in effect, throw mikle hat reasoning and manie interruptiones: "Sir, we will humblie reverence your Majestie alwayes, namlie in publick, but sen we have this occasioun to be with your Majestie in privat, and the treuthe is yie ar brought in extream danger bathe of your lyff and croun, and with yow the countrey and Kirk of Chryst is lyk to wrak, for nocht telling yow the treuthe, and giffen of yow a fathfull counsall, we mon discharge our dewtie thairin, or els be trators bathe to Chryst and yow! And, thairfor, sir, as divers tymes befor, sa now again, I mon tell yow, thair is twa Kings and twa kingdomes in Scotland. Thair is Chryst Jesus the King, and his kingdome the Kirk, whase subject King James the Saxt is, and of whase kingdome nocht a king nor a lord, nor a heid, bot a member!... And, Sir, when yie war in your swadling-cloutes, Chryst Jesus' rang[22] friely in this land in spyt of all his enemies.'"

[Note 22: Reigned.]

The King bent before the tempest of Melville's indignation, and the storm ended in calm: the deputation was dismissed with the promise that the Popish lords would 'get no grace at his hands till they satisfied the Kirk.'

The ministers had learned what value to attach to the royal word, so that they cannot have been greatly surprised when soon afterwards James showed his intention not only to indemnify the excommunicated lords, but to restore them to favour at Court. At this time Huntly's Countess received a special mark of the King's favour in being invited to the baptismal ceremony of his daughter Elizabeth, and at the same time another Popish lady was put in custody of the Princess at the Court.

The ultimate issue of this matter, which was soon involved in another and greater controversy between the Crown and the Church, was that the Popish lords, after a formal submission to the Courts of the Church, were absolved from their excommunication and restored to their former positions. No one believed that there was any sincerity in the transaction either on the part of Huntly and his friends, or of the King and Council, or of the majority of the Assembly: the whole business was concocted and pushed through by the Crown for its own ends, with as much of the semblance of concession to the Church as possible, and as little of the reality. The action of the Court throughout the whole case was such as to breed the greatest suspicion of the King's honesty in professing zeal for the defence of the country from the dangers threatened by Popish intrigues at home and abroad. Even Burton, whom no one will suspect of partiality to the Church, and whose animus against the ministers often overcomes his historic judgment, in writing of what he calls the 'edifying ceremony' of the absolution of the lords, says:

'It must be conceded to their enemies that it was a solemn farce; and
whatever there might be in words or the surface of things, there would
be, when these Earls were restored, a power in the North ready to
co-operate with any Spanish invader.'

CHAPTER VIII

THE KING'S GREEK GIFT TO THE CHURCH

'The words of his mouth were smoother than butter, but war was
in his heart.'

The Psalms.

In 1596, at one of the many conferences which he held with the
Commissioners of the Church on the business with which our last chapter
was concerned, the King disclosed a new policy. For the double purpose
of diverting public attention from the Popish lords, and of starting a
new process for the overthrow of Presbytery, he cast off all disguise
and threw down the gauntlet to the ministers. He told the Commissioners
that the question of the redding of the marches between the two
jurisdictions must be reopened, and that there could be no peace between
him and the Church until it satisfied him on these four points:--that
ministers should make no reference in the pulpit to affairs of
government; that the Courts of the Church should take no cognisance of
offences against the law of the land; that the General Assembly should
only meet by the King's special command; and that the Acts of the
Assembly should, no more than the statutes of the realm, be held valid

till they received his sanction and ratification.

Had these demands been granted, the liberties of the Church would have
been placed under the King's feet, the ministers would have worn a Court
muzzle, and the Assembly would have sat only to register the King's
decrees. With the pulpits silenced in regard to affairs of government
and offences against the law, the country would have been deprived of
the only organ of public opinion that checked the arbitrary power of the
Crown and the prevailing laxity in the administration of justice. Had it
not been for words of 'venturesome edge' spoken from the pulpits on
necessary occasions, we cannot estimate how the liberties of Scotland
would have suffered. We are told by some dispassionate and carefully
balanced readers of Scottish History that the Presbyterian Reformers of
the sixteenth and seventeenth centuries cared no more for liberty than
did their opponents, and that the controversy was between Presbyterian
tyranny on the one hand and Episcopal tyranny on the other; and, of
course, it is to be allowed that *individual* liberty was neither
claimed nor admitted by any party in that age, as it is by all parties
in ours. But the Presbyterian Church was *the nation* in a sense which
held true of no other organisation civil or ecclesiastical--certainly
not of the aristocratic Parliament,--and its courts and pulpits were the
voice of the nation--the only articulate voice it had; so that in
pleading for the rights and liberties of the Church, in demanding for
it free speech and effective influence in the nation's affairs, Melville
and the Presbyterians were, from first to last, fighting for the rights
and liberties of the people against the personal and injurious ambitions
of the King and his courtiers. There can be no really historical
understanding of the course of events in Scotland through the whole
Reforming period except in the light of this truth--that the interests
of Presbytery were dear to the best men in the country, from generation
to generation, because they were the interests both of national
righteousness and of national freedom. That the Church should be free to
reform the nation, meant, practically, and in the only way possible,

that the nation should be free to reform itself. Knox, Melville, and the Covenanters were the nobler sons of Wallace and Bruce, and fought out their battles. And this contest with James was a crucial illustration of the principles involved in the whole long struggle.

On the very day the Commissioners were conferring with the King, it came out that Mr. David Black, minister of St. Andrews, had been summoned before the Council on a charge rising out of sermons he had preached. Black was accused, in the first instance, of having used language disrespectful to Queen Elizabeth. Bowes, the English Ambassador, had been wrought upon by one of the courtiers to make a complaint against Black on this score; and although the latter had made an explanation with which the Ambassador professed himself satisfied, the charge was persisted in. Black was further accused of having, on various occasions, made offensive references to the King and the Queen, and to others of high position in the land. The charges were based on sermons spread over two or three years, a circumstance which of itself suggests that the prosecution had been got up for ulterior government purposes; that it was a 'forged cavillation,' as Bruce called it in his pulpit in Edinburgh.

Black denied all the charges, and declared that they had been concocted by well-known private enemies. When the Council resolved to go on with the prosecution, Black, on the advice of the Commissioners of the Church, declined its jurisdiction. The Council went on with the trial--Black taking no part in it,--found the charges proven, and sentenced him to go into ward beyond the North Water (the North Esk). The same week, the Commissioners of Assembly who had come to Edinburgh to watch the trial were ordered to quit the capital, along with many of their leading supporters among the citizens, within twenty-four hours; and a Proclamation was issued containing a vehement attack on the ministers, and reviving one of the provisions of the Black Acts, which prohibited all preachers from censuring the conduct of the Government or

any of 'the loveabill(!)' Acts of Parliament, required all magistrates
to take measures against any who should be found so doing, and made it a
crime to hear such speeches without reporting them to the authorities.
This Proclamation left the country in no doubt as to the character of
the King's policy towards the Church; for never had even James asserted
his claims to absolute authority, alike in civil and ecclesiastical
affairs, more arrogantly. It declared that the royal power was above all
the estates, spiritual as well as temporal; and that the King was judge
of speeches of whatever quality, uttered in the pulpit.

The citizens of Edinburgh were naturally thrown into violent commotion
by these events; and when their minds were in this inflammable
condition, an incident occurred which brought the public excitement to
its height, and which the Government turned to its own account in
prosecuting its quarrel with the Church with still greater vigour. This
incident is known as 'the Riot of 17th December' (1596). On that day a
number of the ministers and of the nobles who were in sympathy with
them, were assembled for consultation in one of the chapels of St.
Giles', known as the 'Little Church,' when they were startled by some
one near the door raising the shout, 'Fy! save yourselves,' or, as
another version gives it, 'The Papists are in arms to take the town and
cut all your throats.' The Assembly at once broke up, and all made for
the street. The alarm spread through the city, and soon brought the
people in crowds to the High Street, many of them armed; and it is said
that some of them surrounded the Tolbooth, where the King was sitting at
the time with the Council, crying to 'bring out Haman,' and shouting,
'The sword of the Lord and of Gideon.' On hearing of the tumult, the
Provost and the ministers of the city made for the scene, and through
their exertions peace was restored within an hour, and without any one
being hurt.

The man who raised the panic in the 'Little Church' never came to be
known; but it was believed that he was one of the 'Cubiculars' (as they

were called), or gentlemen of the King's bedchamber, who were annoyed at the Octavians, on account of the retrenchments made in the King's household expenditure; and that this *ruse* had been devised for the purpose of fomenting the differences between the Octavians and the ministers.

The action taken by the Court in connection with the riot would have been ridiculous had its consequences for the Church not been so serious. Next day the King removed the Court to Linlithgow, and a Proclamation was made at the Cross of Edinburgh announcing that, owing to the 'treasonable' arming of the citizens, the Courts of Law would also be removed from the city, and ordering the four ministers and several prominent citizens of Edinburgh into ward in the Castle, and citing them before the Council on a general charge. The ministers fled, as Melville and others had done in like circumstances twelve years before.

In January 1597 the King returned to the capital, and the Estates were called together to confirm the Acts passed by the Council for punishing all whom it chose to hold in blame for the riot of the previous month. In accordance with these Acts, all ministers were to be required, on pain of losing their stipends, to subscribe a bond acknowledging the King to be the only judge of those charged with using treasonable language in the pulpit; authorising magistrates to apprehend any preachers who might be found so doing, and declaring the King to have the power of discharging ministers at his pleasure. Vindictive Acts against the city of Edinburgh were also confirmed. Henceforth no General Assembly was to be held within its walls; the seat of the Presbytery was to be transferred to Musselburgh or Dalkeith; the manses of the city ministers were to be forfeit to the Crown; these ministers were not to be readmitted to their pulpits, nor any others chosen in their places without his Majesty's consent; and no magistrates, any more than ministers, were to be appointed without the royal approval.

At the same meeting of the Estates, arrangements were made for the restoration of the Popish lords. The contrast between the King's leniency towards them, and his rigorous and vindictive measures towards the ministers, plainly advertised the disposition of the King to both. Well might Robert Bruce ask in one of his sermons--'What sall the religius of both countries think of this? Is this the moyen to advance the Prince's grandeur and to turne the hearts of the people towards his Hienesse?' Spirited protests were made by the Commissioners of the Church; they did not mince their language--'We deteast that Act ... making the King head of the Kirk ... as High Treason and sacriledge against Christ the onlie King and Head of the Kirk.' The magistrates did not show the same mettle, but made submission on all the points required.

Emboldened by the effect of these measures, the King lost no time in pressing forward his designs against the Church. His next step was to issue a state paper containing a long series of questions which should reopen discussion on the established policy, and convening a meeting of the representatives of the Church and of the Estates for the purpose of debating and deciding on these questions. The ministers at once began preparations for the struggle; and it was Melville's Synod--always the Church's pilot in the storm--that once more took the lead. It appointed Commissioners to urge the King to abandon the proposed Convention, and to refer the business to a regular meeting of Assembly. Should the King refuse this request, the Commissioners were not to acknowledge the Convention as a lawful meeting of the Assembly, nor to admit its claim to enter on the Constitution of the Church. In any private discussion they were strenuously to oppose any movement on the part of the King to disturb the existing order.

The Convention met in Perth on the last day of February 1597. In anticipation, the King, knowing well the determined opposition he would encounter at the hands of those ministers who regularly attended the

Assembly and took part in its business, had despatched one of his courtiers, Sir Patrick Murray, to do the part of 'Whip' among the ministers north of the Tay, and so to pack the Assembly with members who rarely attended it, who were unaccustomed to its business, and who were more likely to be facile for the King's purposes than their brethren in the south. Murray--'the Apostle of the North,' as he was sarcastically called--brought the Highland ministers down in droves, poisoned their minds with jealousy of the southern ministers, and flattered them with the assurance of the King's esteem.

After a debate, lasting for three days, the majority agreed to hold the Convention as a meeting of the Assembly. Thereafter the King's questions were entered upon, and so far discussed, when the business was adjourned to another meeting to be held in Dundee. In agreeing to recognise the Convention as an Assembly, and to open up the subject of its own constitution, the Church came down from its only safe position, and virtually delivered itself into the King's hands, thereby inflicting a wound on its own liberties, from which it took a whole century to recover. That surrender was the letting in of waters, and henceforth the Assemblies were the organ of the Crown rather than of the Church--'Whar Chryst gydit befor, the Court began then to govern all; whar pretching befor prevalit, then polecie tuk the place; and, finalie, whar devotioun and halie behaviour honoured the Minister, then began pranking at the chare, and prattling in the ear of the Prince, to mak the Minister to think him selff a man of estimatioun!... The end of the Assemblies of auld was, whow Chryst's Kingdome might stand in halines and friedome: now, it is whow Kirk and Relligioun may be framed to the polytic esteat of a frie Monarchie, and to advance and promot the grandour of man, and supream absolut authoritie in all causes, and over all persones, alsweill Ecclesiasticall as Civill.'

The Dundee Assembly met in May; again the northern ministers were present in force; and again every means the Court could contrive was

used to win over the members, and especially those of mark among them.
Melville came to attend the Assembly; and one evening before it met, Sir
Patrick Murray sent for the younger Melville, and urged him to advise
his uncle to go home, as, if he did not, the King would order him to be
removed. On receiving the answer that it would be useless to give
Melville such advice, since the threat of death would not turn him from
his duty, Sir Patrick rejoined, 'Surely I fear he suffer the dint of the
King's wrath.' James Melville told his uncle of the interview with the
King's 'Whip.' What his uncle's answer was, 'I need not wraite,' he
says. On the morning of the Assembly the Melvilles were summoned by the
King. The interview went on smoothly till they entered on the business
for which the Assembly was called, when 'Mr. Andro brak out with his
wounted humor of fredome and zeall and ther they heeled on, till all the
hous, and clos bathe, hard mikle of a large houre.' Melville was much
too stormy a courtier for the King's purposes.

At the Dundee Assembly, the transactions at the Perth Convention were
confirmed; and thereafter a new proposal was made by the King and
carried, which was fraught with evil for the Church. This was the
appointment of an extraordinary standing Commission to confer with the
King on the Church's affairs--a Commission which came to be a kind of
King's Council set up in the Assembly. Calderwood speaks of it as the
King's 'led horse,' and James Melville calls it 'the very neidle to draw
in the Episcopall threid.'

Armed with his new provisions, the King immediately began to use them
with energy. Edinburgh and St. Andrews were the strongholds of the
Church, where the Invincibles in its ministry were chiefly found. The
ministers of the former had already been disposed of, and the King's
next move was directed against those of the latter--above all, against
Melville, the chief Invincible. The two leading ministers of St.
Andrews, Black and Wallace, were discharged; George Gledstanes, who
afterwards became a Bishop, being appointed in Black's place; and

Melville was deprived of the Rectorship of the University. At the same time, a law was enacted depriving professors of their seats in Church Courts, the object being, of course, to exclude Melville, whose influence in the Courts was so commanding.

At the end of this year another step was taken towards the re-erection of Episcopacy. The Commissioners of Assembly, who were now mere creatures of the King, appeared before Parliament, petitioning it to give the Church the right of representation, so as to restore it to its former position as the Third Estate of the realm; proposing also, that for this end the prelatic order should be revived, and the Bishops chosen as the Church's representatives. The jurisdiction of the prelates within the Church was to be left over for future consideration, in accordance with James's policy, which was not to filch so much of the Church's liberty at any one time as might frustrate his hope of taking it all away in the end. The petition of the Commissioners was granted by the Parliament.

In February of the following year, 1598, the Synod of Fife met, Sir Patrick Murray being present as the King's Commissioner; and the Court at once entered on the question of the hour, Should the Church agree to send representatives to Parliament? James Melville, who was the first to rise and address the House, protested against their falling to work to 'big up' bishops, whom all their days they had been 'dinging doun.' Andrew Melville followed, and supported his nephew's counsel in his own vehement manner. David Ferguson, the oldest minister of the Church, who had been at its planting in 1560, rose and warned the House of the fatal gift that was offered by the King. John Davidson, another venerable and influential member of the Synod, made a powerful speech, concluding with the same warning: 'Busk, busk, busk him as bonnilie as ye can, and fetche him in als fearlie as yie will, we sie him weill aneuche, we sie the horns of his mytre.' When the Synod met, the majority were inclined to favour the proposal; but these speeches, greatly to the chagrin of the Royal Commissioner, turned the feeling of the House.

The same business occupied the next Assembly, which met in Dundee in March. Melville having come to the Assembly in defiance of the recent Act depriving him of his seat, the King challenged his commission in the Court. Melville replied with great spirit; and before he was discharged, delivered his views on the King's policy. John Davidson boldly defended his leader's right to sit in the Assembly, and, turning to the King, told him that he had his seat there as a Christian man, and not as President of the Court. Next day Davidson complained again of the treatment Melville had received, openly ascribing it to the King's fear of his opposition. 'I will not hear a word on that head,' James burst forth.--'Then,' said Davidson, 'we must crave help of Him that will hear us.' Not only was Melville excluded from the Assembly, but its business was not allowed to proceed till he left the town, lest he should stiffen the brethren who resorted to him for advice against the King's proposals. The royal measures were, after all, only carried by ten votes; and even that majority would not have been secured had the King not declared, with his usual disingenuousness, that he had no intention of restoring the bishops as a spiritual order, but only as representatives of the Church in Parliament.

It was decided that the number of representatives should correspond with that of the old prelates, and that they should be chosen conjointly by the King and the Assembly. When, however, the House proceeded to details, so much difference of opinion arose, that the King thought it prudent to adjourn. The questions were referred to the inferior Courts for their consideration, and thereafter each Synod was to appoint three commissioners to confer on the subject before the King along with all the theological professors.

This conference was held, and was packed with the King's men. In many cases the delegates were not the choice of those they represented. The

trick by which this was effected was in keeping with the rest of the
King's conduct in the business. In many of the presbyteries the
Invincibles were placed upon the leets from which the commissioners were
to be elected; they thus lost their votes, and those who remained to
make the choice chose the delegates desired by the King.

Melville attended the conference, and opposed the King at every point.
On the question of the duration of the office of the representatives,
there was a very lively piece of repartee between the two. Melville had
been contending that the King's proposal to appoint the representatives
for life would establish lordship over the brethren, 'tyme strynthning
opinioun and custome confirming conceat,' when the King broke in upon
his speech with the remark that 'there was na thing sa guid bot might be
bathe ill suspected and abbusit, and sa we suld be content with na
thing.' Melville retorted that they 'doubted of the guidness, and had
ower just cause to suspect the evill of it.' The King's next thrust
was: 'There was na fault bot we [the ministers] war all trew aneuche to
the craft,' which Melville turned with the remark, 'But God make us all
trew aneuche to Christ say we.'--'The ministers,' said the King, 'sould
ly in contempt and povertie [if their status was not raised as he
proposed].--'It was their Maister's case before them,' rejoined
Melville; 'it may serve them weill aneuche to be as he was, and better
povertie with sinceritie nor promotioun with corruptioun.'--'Uthers
would be promovit to that room in Parliament,' said the King [his
Majesty could not want his three estates], 'wha wald opres and wrak his
Kirk.'--Melville answered: 'Let Chryst the King and advenger of the
wrangs done to his Kirk and them deal togidder as he hes done before;
let see wha gettes the warst.'--Once more the King argued: 'Men wald be
that way [by a temporary appointment] disgraced, now sett upe and now
sett by and cast down and sa discouragit from doing guid,' when Melville
concluded: 'He that thinks it disgrace to be employed in what God's Kirk
thinks guid, hes lytle grace in him; for grace is given to the lowlie.'

Another point was the name to be given to the representatives. Arguing against the King's proposal to style them bishops, Melville used great freedom of speech: 'The nam [Greek: episkopos] being a Scripture nam, might be giffen tham, provyding, that because ther was sum thing mair put to the mater of a Bischope's office then the Word of God could permit, it sould have a lytle eik[23] put to the nam quhilk the Word of God joyned to it, and sa it war best to baptize tham with the nam that Peter i. cap. iv. giffes to sic lyk officers, calling tham [Greek: allotrioepiskopous], war nocht they wald think scham to be merschallit with sic as Peter speakes of ther, viz., murderers, theiffs, and malefactors?' Melville was much pleased with his own wit: 'Verilie that gossop [this was Andro] at the baptisme (gif sa that I dar play with that word) was no a little vokie[24] for getting of the bern's name,' We hardly understand Melville unless we take into account the spirit almost of glee with which he fought 'the good fight'; he was 'always a fighter,' not purely from stress of circumstances, but because he had it in him; he was never quarrelsome, and he needed a high issue to rouse him--but that given, he sniffed the battle from far, and dearly loved to be in the thick of it.

[Note 23: Addition.]

[Note 24: Vain.]

The questions were then left to be disposed of by the General Assembly, the King warning the members of the conference before it broke up that, whatever the Assembly might do, he would have his Third Estate restored.

By this time the country had learned, by the publication of the King's two books-- **The True Law of Free Monarchy** and the Basilicon Doron--that James's practice in the government of the nation and in his policy towards the Church was in accordance with his theory of kingship. By a 'Free Monarchy' he meant, not a monarchy in which the people are

free, but in which the King is free from all control of the people. He
claimed that the King was above the law; and that 'as it is atheism and
blasphemy to dispute what God can do, so it is presumption and a high
contempt in a subject to dispute what a King can do, or to say that a
King cannot do this or that.'

In the **Basilicon Doron** he unveiled his real feelings and designs with
regard to Presbytery, which, at the very time he was writing, he was
professing to respect--declaring that the ruling of the Kirk was no
small part of the King's office; that parity among the ministers could
not agree with a monarchy; that Puritans were pests in the Kirk and
commonwealth of Scotland, and that bishops must be set up.

The General Assembly met in Montrose in March 1600; and Melville, who
had come to the town to attend it, was commanded by the King to keep to
his room. Summoned to his Majesty's presence, he was asked why he was
giving trouble in attending the Assembly after the Act depriving him of
his seat; when he replied: 'He had a calling in his Kirk of God and of
Jesus Christ, the King of Kings, quhilk he behovit to dischairge at all
occasiounes, being orderlie callit thereto, as he wes at this time; and
that for feir of a grytter punischment then could any earthly king
inflict.' The King in anger uttered a threat, when Melville, putting his
hand to his head, said: 'Sir, it is this that ye would haiff. Ye sall
haiff it: Tak it! Tak it! or ye bereave us of the liberties of Jesus
Christ and His kingdome.'

Excluded from the Assembly, Melville remained in Montrose during the
sittings, to assist his brethren with his counsel. The King was present
at every sitting, and was busy from early morning till late at night
canvassing the members of the House; and though there were many who
stood honestly by their principles, his authority and diplomacy carried
the day. The House was so far from being favourable to the King's
scheme, that it would have thrown it out, but for his arbitrary closure

of the debate; it did throw out the proposal of life representatives; and it safeguarded the other clauses of the measure with so many *caveats*, that had they been observed, it could not have served for the restoration of the bishops. These *caveats*, however, were not observed; then, as many a time before and since in Scotland, the Church got the worst of the bargain in seeking a compromise with the civil power, and found too late that she had sold her birthright. In less than a month after the Assembly rose, three of the ministers had been appointed to bishoprics, and these ministers took their seats in the next Parliament. We have seen that James, whenever he felt that the tide of hostile opinion in the country was becoming too strong for him, sought to turn it by some popular act. The General Assembly held in Burntisland in May 1601 witnessed one of those periodic fits of apparent yielding, on the King's part, to the will of the nation. He was in peculiar disfavour at the time, owing to the mysterious tragedy which took place at Gowrie House in August 1600. There was a widespread, deep-rooted suspicion that the Earl of that name, who was a favourite of the people, and the head of a Protestant house, had been the victim rather than the author of the conspiracy; and the public irritation was increased by the new quarrel which James forced on Bruce and the other ministers of Edinburgh for refusing to repeat, in the thanksgiving service appointed to be held for his preservation, his own version of the story. At the Burntisland Assembly the King appeared and made humble confession of the shortcomings of his Government, especially in respect of his indulgence of the Papists, and gave lavish promises of amendment.

Two years afterwards, before leaving Scotland to ascend the English throne, these promises were renewed; but, as usual with James, they were only the prelude of greater oppression. His threat to the Puritan ministers at Hampton Court conference--that he would 'harry them out of the country'--left their brethren of the Scottish Church in no doubt as to the course he would pursue towards themselves, now that he had attained to a position of so much greater authority.

The Assembly was the ***palladium*** of the Church's liberty; and the policy which the King had begun before leaving Scotland, of usurping the government of the Church by gaining the control of the Assembly, was vigorously prosecuted after his accession to the throne of England. The meetings were prorogued again and again by royal authority, but always under protest from the most independent of the ministers. For their zeal in promoting a petition to him on the subject, the King ordered the two Melvilles to be imprisoned; but the Scottish Council dared not lay hands on them in view of the unpopularity of the Government. In the year 1605 the quarrel between the King and the ministers over the right of free Assembly came to a head. A meeting appointed to be held in Aberdeen had been prorogued by the King's authority for a second time, and prorogued ***sine die***. The ministers felt that if they acquiesced in so grave a violation of the law of the Church, her liberty would be irrecoverably lost; several of the Presbyteries accordingly resolved to send representatives to Aberdeen to hold the Assembly in defiance of the King's prohibition. This was done, and the House had no sooner been constituted than a King's messenger appeared and commanded the members to disperse; whereupon the Moderator dissolved the Assembly and fixed a day for its next meeting. The law-officers of the Crown were immediately instructed to prosecute the ministers who had attended, and fourteen of them were tried and sentenced to imprisonment--two of them, Forbes the Moderator and John Welch, Knox's son-in-law, being sent to Blackness. Six of them having declined the jurisdiction of the Council, were tried for high treason by a packed jury, and found guilty by a majority. So great was the indignation felt throughout the country at the prosecution and the manner in which it had been conducted, that the Council had to inform the King that the Court could not go on with the trial of the others. Eight of the condemned ministers were banished to the Highlands and Islands; and the six who had been found guilty of treason were sent to Blackness and then banished to France. In all the proceedings against those who had made such a manly stand in defence of the Church's liberties, Melville identified himself with his brethren, did all that was in his power to procure their acquittal, and after their sentence visited them in prison.

The King now took another step in his campaign against Presbytery. He ordered all the synods of the Church to meet, in order to have articles submitted to them which provided that the bishops should have full jurisdiction over the ministers, under his Majesty, and that the King should be acknowledged supreme ruler of the Church under Christ. These articles were rejected by Melville's synod, and referred to the Assembly by the others. A meeting of Parliament was summoned to pass the articles into law, and to this Parliament Melville was sent by his presbytery to watch over the interests of the Church. It having been ascertained that it was the King's intention to propose that the statute of the year 1587, annexing the temporalities of the prelates to the Crown, should be repealed, and that the bishops should be restored to their ancient prerogatives and dignities, the ministers lodged a protest beforehand, with Melville's name at the head of the signatories; and when the measure came to be adopted by Parliament, and Melville rose up to renew his protest, he was commanded to leave the House, 'quhilk nevertheless he did not, till he had maid all that saw and heard him understand his purpose.' Melville seldom failed in any circumstances to make those who saw and heard him understand his purpose, and when that was done his end was served.

Among the writings issued at this time against the King's measure, there was one in which it was said of bishops in general, that 'for one preaching made to the people [they] ryde fourtie posts to court; and for a thought or word bestowed for the weal of anie soule care an hundreth for their apparrill, their train ... and goucked gloriosity.'[25] The part taken by the bishops at the opening of this Parliament showed that the new Scottish prelates were likely to verify this indictment against their order. 'The first day of the Ryding in Parliament betwix the Erles and the Lords raid the Bischopes, all in silk and velvet fuit-mantelles, by paires, tuo and tuo, and Saint Androis, the great Metropolitanne, alone by him selff, and are of the Ministeres of no small quantitie, named Arthur Futhey, with his capp at his knie, walkit at his stirrope alongst the streit. But the second day, for not haiffing their awen place as the Papist Bisschoppis of auld had, unto quhois place and dignitie they wer now restorit fully in judgment, quhilk wes befoir the Erles, nixt eftir the Marquesses, thai would not ryde at all, but went to the House of Parliament quyetlie on fuit. This maid the Nobillmen to take up thair presumeing honour, and detest thame, as soon as they had maid thame and sett thame up, perceiving that thair upelyfting wes thair awin douncasting.'

[Note 25: Foolish pomp.]

The Parliament had restored Episcopacy, but the Assembly had not yet wholly succumbed. To secure this end, and so to give to what was entirely his own despotic act the appearance of a change desired by the Church itself, was the King's next aim. And this opens up one of the most disgraceful chapters in the history of James's relations with the Scottish Church.

CHAPTER IX

MELVILLE AT HAMPTON COURT

'But who, if he be called upon to face
Some awful moment to which Heaven has joined
Great issues, good or bad, for human kind,
  Is happy as a lover.'

The Happy Warrior.

A month before the meeting of the Perth Parliament, viz. in May 1606, Melville and his nephew, together with other six ministers, received a letter from the King, commanding them to go to London to confer with him on the affairs of the Church. The letter was very vaguely worded; but it was apparent that James's purpose was either to secure their capitulation to Episcopacy, or to deprive them of all further opportunity of resisting it. The ministers were much perplexed as to whether they should go or stay, but at last they decided to face all risks and obey the King's summons.

On reaching London at the end of August (1606), they got a warm welcome from many ministers in the city who were friendly to their cause. They were offered hospitality by their Graces of Canterbury and York, but they declined a meeting with these prelates till they had seen the King. They soon learned that the King's object in bringing them to London was that they might be set to the public discussion of the affairs of the Church. This the ministers, for many good reasons, were resolved not to do: they could be no parties to any proceedings which brought into question the Church's discipline, and they had no warrant for taking part in such proceedings. With whom were they to hold debate? The English prelates could find within their own Church those who would take them up in regard to the merits of their ecclesiastical system: and the two Scottish archbishops who had come to London to be present at the conference between the King and the eight brethren, could not open their mouths against Presbytery, as the ministers had brought with them documents, in which these prelates had bound themselves to maintain the established constitution of the Presbyterian Church.

The ministers were nearly a month in London before they met the King, who had been making a tour in England. The first interview between them took place at Hampton Court on 20th September. The King was in good humour, and very familiar; he bantered James Balfour on the length to which his beard had grown since they last met in Edinburgh, and was gracious all round.

Next day was the Sabbath, when they were all enjoined by the King to attend a service in the Royal Chapel, to be conducted by Dr. Barlow, Bishop of Rochester. They had been brought to London to be schooled into conformity; and as part of the process, the English bishops had been commanded to prepare a series of sermons for their benefit. These were such a travesty on the texts of Scripture they were supposed to expound, that if they had been addressed to the ministers' own congregations in Scotland, the humblest of their hearers would have resented them. Whatever these bishops could do, they certainly could not preach. They belonged to that section of the clergy who disparage the preacher's function in comparison with the priest's, and who in their own practice do a great deal to bring the former into something like contempt. If the sermons preached before the eight brethren did not convince or edify them, they at least amused them, and gave them practice in the Christian virtue of patience. Dr. Barlow's was not the worst, though his hearers regarded it as an admirable '***confutation***' of the text. The preacher, among the four, who reached the climax of

absurdity was Dr. Andrewes, Bishop of Chichester. He was one of the
extreme High Churchmen of his time: no man urged the doctrine of passive
obedience to a more abject degree, or did more to support with the
sanction of religion the most extravagant pretensions of the Crown. It
was Andrewes who at the Hampton Court Conference declared that James was
inspired by God--the same man who made it his nightly prayer, as he
tells us himself, that he might be preserved from adulating the King! Of
all the sermons preached to, or rather *at*, the eight brethren, his,
as we have said, was the most preposterous, consisting as it did of a
deduction of the King's right to call Assemblies of the Church, from the
passage in Numbers which describes the blowing of the trumpets by the
sons of Aaron to summon the congregation to the tabernacle! Well might a
Scottish lord, who heard Andrewes preach before the Court on the
occasion of James's visit to Scotland in 1617, say of him as he did,
when asked his opinion by the King, that he played with his text rather
than preached upon it. The last of the series of the discourses was the
most candid, and pointed most directly to the object at which they were
all aiming; for the preacher reached the close of the attack upon the
Presbyterians by turning round to the King and exclaiming, 'Downe, downe
with them all!'

On Monday, 22nd September, the ministers were brought to confer with the
King in presence of the Scottish Council. Two points for discussion came
up: First, the proceedings of the Aberdeen Assembly; and, second, the
proposed holding of an Assembly in which order and peace might be
restored to the Church. James Melville spoke for the brethren with great
courtesy, and at the same time with great decision. He declined, in name
of all, to discuss these questions till they had had an opportunity for
consultation among themselves. Other matters were brought forward by the
King, but not formally discussed. One of these was a letter that had
been addressed by James Melville, from his sick-bed, to the Synod of
Fife, in regard to the articles in which the King claimed supremacy in
ecclesiastical affairs. "'I hard, Mr. James Melvill," said the King,

"that ye wreitt a Lettre to the Synod of Fyff at Cowper, quhairin was meikle of Chryst, but lytle guid of the King. Be God I trow ye wes reavand or mad (for he spak so) ye speek utherwayis now. Now, wes that a charitabill judgment of me?"--"Sir," says Mr. James, with a low courtessie, "I wes baith seik and sair in bodie quhan I wreit that Lettre, bot sober and sound in mind. I wreit of your Majestie all guid, assureing my selff and the Bretherine that thais Articles quhairoff a copy cam in my handis could not be from your Majestie, they wer so strange; and quhom sould I think, speik, or wryt guid of, if not of your Majestie, quho is the man under Chryst quhom I wisch most guid and honour unto.'"

At the consultation held among the brethren in regard to the points raised, they decided that when the conference was resumed they would give their answer through one of their number; and that, as to the first question before them, they would decline, for reasons which we need not rehearse, to give any judgment on the Aberdeen Assembly. Meanwhile, however, the King had resolved that each of the ministers should answer the questions for himself, in the hope that their answers would prove conflicting, and so give him an advantage.

At the second conference there were present the members of the English Council, the most eminent of the prelates, and the most illustrious of the nobles. On the King's right hand sat the Primate, with many of England's proudest earls and all the great ministers of state; on his left the young Prince Henry, with the Scottish nobles and councillors; behind the arras several other nobles and bishops were gathered. In the midst of the assemblage stood the eight Scottish ministers, unabashed by the glitter of rank and royalty--plain men decorated with no honours, but in intellect and dignity of character the peers of the best in that company; and to the crowd of courtiers gathered that day in the Council Hall of England they taught a lesson in one of the duties owing to a sovereign which few courtiers have practised--the duty of telling him the truth.

The subject of conference was, as we have said, the conduct of the ministers who had held the Assembly in Aberdeen. The first to be asked their opinion by the King were the Scottish bishops and councillors, who answered promptly and unanimously that 'they had ever damnit that Assembly.' Turning from them to the eight brethren, and addressing their chief--the man above all others whom James sought to entrap: '"Now, Siris," sayis the King, "quhat say ye, and first Mr. Andro Melvill?" Quho, with meikle low courtessie, talkit all his mynd in his awin maner, roundly, soundly, fully, freely, and fervently, almaist the space of ane hour, not omitting any poynt he could remember.' James Balfour was the next called on, and the King, by the time he was done with Melville and him, evidently realised that he was getting the worst of the encounter--'smelling how the matter went, he seemit weary.' Balfour was followed by James Melville, who at the close of his examination had the courage to hand to the King a supplication addressed to him by the condemned ministers, which James received with an angry smile. Next came Scott, whose speech was 'ane prettie piece of logicall and legal reasouneing, quhilk delighted and moved the judicious audiens.' The rest followed 'all most reverently on kneis, but thairwith most friely, statly, and plainely, to the admiration of the English auditorie, quho wer not accustomit to heir the King so talkit to and reassounit with.' When all had been examined, Melville craved to be heard again, and had the last word: he 'spake out in his awin maner, and friely and plainely affirmit the innocence of thais guid, faithfull, and honest Britherin, in all thair proceidingis at Abirdein; and thairfoir he recomptit the wrongis done unto thame at Linlithgow, as ane that wes present as an eye and ear witness; and taking him in direct termes to the Advocat, Mr. Thomas Hammiltoune, he invyit scharpely againes him, telling him planely and pathetically, of his favouring and spaireing the Papistis, and craftie, cruell, and malicious dealing againes the Ministeres of Jesus Chryst; so that he could have done no moir againes the saints of God

then he had at Linlithgow! At the quhilk words the King luiking to the
Archbisschoppes, sayis, "Quhat? Me thinkis he makes him the Antichryst!"
And, suddentlie, again with ane oath, "Be God! It is the divelis name
in the Revelatioune! He hes maid the divel of him, welbelovit
Bretherine, brother Johne!" And so, cuttitly ryseing, and turneing his
back, he sayes, "God be with yow, Siris!"' As the King was moving out of
the Presence Chamber he turned round and asked what remedy the Eight
proposed for the jars of the Church, when they all as with one voice
replied, 'A free Assembly!'

While on their way from Hampton Court to their lodgings in Kingston, the
Eight were recalled and charged not to return to Scotland, or to come
near the King or Court until they were sent for. After this they enjoyed
a short holiday--'we had three dayis to refresche us and relax our
myndis dureing the quhilk we wer visiting the fieldis about, namely,
Nonsuche and Richmont.'

Monday, 29th September, being Michaelmas Day, an elaborate service was
held in the King's Chapel, the two Melvilles being present by the King's
command. The younger suspected, rightly as it proved, that the King's
object was to try their patience and provoke his uncle to an outburst of
indignation which might bring him into trouble. The service was so high
that a German visitor at the English Court declared it was not a whit
behind the solemnity of the Mass but for the absence of the adoration of
the Host. The snare set for Melville on this occasion succeeded, for it
was a satirical verse on this service that was afterwards made the
pretext for sending him to prison.

After the service, the Eight were summoned before the Scottish Council,
convened in the house of the Earl of Dunbar. They were called in, one by
one, and once more questioned as to their approval of the Aberdeen
Assembly. James Melville, who was the first called, made a patriotic
speech, protesting warmly against the trial of Scotsmen on English soil

and by English law; the others followed him in the same strain. His
uncle was the last to be called, and he 'gaiff thame enought of it, alse
plainely and scharplie as he wes accustomit, namely, telling thame
flattly, that they knew not quhat they did; and wer degenerat from the
antiant nobilitie of Scotland, quho wer wont to give thair landis and
lyffes for the fridom of the Kingdome and Gospel, and they wer bewraying
and ovirturneing the same! Till it became laite, and eftir sune-sett,
that they were faine to dimitt us to the nixt calling for.'

On the 2nd of October, the Eight were called again before the Scottish
Council, and questions put to them bearing still on the same subject, to
which they gave the same answers. The King, in fact, was only marking
time to detain Melville and his colleagues in London till he had
'effecuate matteres at home' according to his mind.

For a month the ministers were not asked to appear again in Court; the
session of Parliament had begun, and the King was engaged with the
business of the Legislature. During this time they all lived together,
and their lodging was the resort of many of their Puritan brethren in
the city and neighbourhood. They had much 'guid exercise' in the Word
and in prayer. But the King and the Bishops having set spies on them who
reported the way in which they were spending their time, they were all
commanded to go into ward--each with a separate bishop. Andrew
Melville's gaoler-in-lawn was to be the Bishop of Winchester, and his
nephew's the Bishop of Durham; but the two made such a spirited protest
to the King, that his command was not meanwhile enforced.

On the last day of November--it was a Sabbath--Melville, with his nephew
and Wallace, was summoned to Whitehall to answer for certain Latin
verses which had come into the King's hand. These were the lampoon which
Melville had made on the Michaelmas service in the Royal Chapel, and he
at once acknowledged the authorship. Interrupted in his apology by the
Primate, Bancroft, who presided in the absence of the King, and who

denounced his offence as treason, he turned upon him the torrent of his invective. 'My lords,' exclaimed he, 'Andrew Melville was never a traitor. But, my lords, there was one Richard Bancroft (let him be sought for) who, during the life of the late Queen, wrote a treatise against his Majesty's title to the Crown of England; and *here*' (pulling the *corpus delicti* from his pocket) 'is the book which was answered by my brother, John Davidson.' While Bancroft was stunned and silenced by the impetuosity of the attack, Melville went on to charge him with the chief responsibility for the Romish ritual that had been introduced into the English Church, and for the silencing of the Puritan ministers; and then taking him by the white sleeves of his rochet, he shook them 'in his maner frielie and roundlie, and called them Romish rags and the mark of the Beast.' The Primate was the reputed author of a book attacking Presbytery, and entitled The English Scottizing for Genevan Discipline. Melville denounced him as having proved himself in that work 'the Capital Enemy of all the Reformed Churches of Europe, whom he would oppose to the effusion of the last drop of blood in his body, and whom it was a constant grief to him to see at the head of the King's Council in England.' He next turned his invective on another prelate present--Barlow--who in writing on the Hampton Court Conference had spoken of the King as in the Kirk of Scotland, but not of it: he marvelled that the Bishop had been left unpunished 'for making the King of no religion.' He was just beginning to put the rapier of his satire into the four sermons preached in the Royal Chapel against Presbytery, when he was interrupted by a Scottish nobleman present. 'Remember,' said he, 'where you are and to whom you are speaking.'--'I remember it very well, my lord,' retorted Melville, 'and am only sorry that your lordship, by sitting here and countenancing such proceedings against me, should furnish a precedent which may yet be used against yourself or your posterity.'

An hour after the close of this memorable scene, the Eight were recalled, and Melville was admonished by the Lord Chancellor and

ordered to go into ward, at his Majesty's pleasure, with the Dean of St.
Paul's; the others were 'commandit to the custodie of their ain wyse and
discreit cariage.' A warrant was at the same time issued by the Council
to the Dean, enjoining him to give no one access to his prisoner, and to
do his utmost to convert him to Episcopacy. To the Dean's house,
accordingly, Melville went, and he remained there till the following
March.

In that month the King renewed his order to the other ministers to take
up their lodgings, each in a bishop's house. James Melville again sent a
protest to the clerk of the Council; he also saw both the Bishop of
Durham and the Primate on the business; and his accounts of the
interviews are very piquant. In his visit to the Primate he was
accompanied by Scott. Bancroft received them with great deference, and
sought to impress them with the King's courtesy in desiring that they
should be entertained by the highest of the clergy. James Melville
answered, with much dignity, that compulsory courtesy was agreeable to
no man; that the Scottish ministers were more acustomed to bestowing
hospitality than receiving it; and that with such contrary opinions as
they held on matters of Church and State, the bishops would not be
pleasant hosts, and as little would the ministers be pleasant guests.
Bancroft was frank enough to admit, that it was more to meet the wishes
of the King than to please themselves that he and the other prelates
offered entertainment to the ministers: he was, in truth, afraid that
the latter, with their scrupulous notions, would prove dull guests and
be offended at the games of cards and other diversions with which the
lords of the Anglican Church were in the habit of passing their social
hours. The conversation then turned to the pet project of the King--the
conforming of the Scottish Church to Episcopacy. James Melville,
speaking in his own mild way, was listened to with patience by the
Primate; but when Scott began to enter into the subject in a
characteristically Scottish fashion, with great seriousness and
elaboration, Bancroft's patience failed him; and interrupting his

discourse, smiling and laying his hand on his shoulder, the Primate said, 'Tush, man! Tak heir a coupe of guid seck.' And therewith filling the cup, he made them both drink, and after a little mild conviviality the two ministers left the Palace.

At the end of March the chief prisoner received an order from the Council to transfer himself to the custody of the Bishop of Winchester. He left the Dean's, but *forgot* to go to the Bishop's, and for two months his evasion of the Council's instruction was winked at, and he lodged with the other brethren. The last act in this prolonged drama was now to be performed, and the King's part in it was characteristically base. Early in the morning of Sabbath, 26th April, one of the Earl of Salisbury's servants came to Melville at his lodging in Bow with an urgent message to him to meet the Earl at Whitehall early on the same day. Melville had no suspicion that the Premier had summoned him for any unfriendly purpose, and at once, borrowing his landlord's horse, posted off to Court. He took a moment to look in on his nephew, who suspected that he was to be called again before the Council, and who, as soon as his uncle left, followed on foot to the Palace with other two of the ministers. The Premier did not keep his appointment; and Melville, tired of waiting, came to the inn at Westminster, where he knew that his nephew and other two brethren were to dine, and joined them in their meal: 'And quhill our buird coverit,[26] and the meitt put thairon, he uttirit to us ane excellent meditatioun, quhilk he had walking in the gallerie, on the second Psalme, joyneing thairwith prayer; quhairby we wer all muche movit; accounting the same in place of our Sabbath foirnoone's exercise, endit, and, sitting doun to dinner, he rehersit his St. Georgis Verses, with vehement invectioun againes the corruptiounes and superstitiounes of England. Thairfoir, his cousine, Mr. James, says to him, "Remember Ovidis verses--

'Si saperem, doctas odissem jure sorores
  Numina cultori perniciosa suo!'"

[Note 26: While our table was being spread.]

His answer was in the verses following:--

> "Sed nunc (tanta meo comes est insania morbo)
> Saxa (malum!) refero rursus ad icta pedem."

"Weill," sayis his cousine, "eit your dinner, and be of good courage, for I sall warrand yow ye sal be befoir the Council for your Verses."--"Weill," sayis he, "my heart is full and burdened, and I will be glaid to haif ane occasioun to disburdein it, and speik all my mynd plainely to thame for the dishonouring of Chryst, and wraik of sua many soulis for their doeings; be the beiring doun the sinceritie and fridom of the Gospel, stoping that healthsome breath of Godis mouth, and maintaining of the Papistis' corruptiounes and superstitiounes."--"I warrand you," sayis Mr. James, "they know you will speik your mynd friely; and thairfoir, hes concludit to make that a meines to keip yow from going home to Scotland."--He answered, "Iff God hes ony thing to doe with me in Scotland more, He will bring me home to Scotland again iff He haiff any service for me: giff not, let me glorifie Him, quhidder or quhairever I be; and as I haif said often to yow, cousine, I think God hes sume pairt to play with us on this theatre!" We had not half dyneit quhen one comes to him from Lord Salisberie; to quhom he said, "Sir, I waitted longe upon my Lordis dinner till I waxed verie hungrie, and could not stay longer. I pray my Lord to suffir me to tak a lytle of my awin dinner!" That messenger wes not weill gone quhill againe comes another; soone eftir that, Mr. Alexander Hay, the Scottish Secretar, telling him that the Counsel was long sett attending him. At the heiring quhairoff, with great motioun, raysing, he prayit; and, leiving us at diner (for we wer expressely chairgit that we come not within the Police), went with Mr. Alexander Hay, with great commotioun of mynd.' Within an hour of Melville's leaving them, a messenger whom they had

sent to ascertain the result of the Council meeting returned with tears
in his eyes to announce that their Chief had been conveyed to the Tower.

The proceedings at the Council we learn from the French Ambassador at
the English Court. The King did not appear in the Council Chamber, but
was in close attendance at the keyhole of the next apartment. 'The Earl
of Salisbury took up the subject, and began to reprove him for his
obstinacy in refusing to acknowledge the Primacy, and for the verses
which he had made in derision of the Royal Chapel. Melville was so
severe in his reply both in what related to the King and to the Earl
personally, that his lordship was completely put to silence. To his
assistance came the Archbishop of Canterbury, then the Earl of
Northampton, then the Lord Treasurer; all of whom he rated in such a
manner, sparing none of the vices, public or private, with which they
are respectively taxed (and none of them are angels), that they would
have been glad that he had been in Scotland. In the end, not being able
to induce him to swear to the Primacy, and not knowing any other way to
revenge themselves on him, they agreed to send him prisoner to the
Tower. When the sentence was pronounced, he exclaimed: "To this comes
the boasted pride of England! A month ago you put to death a priest, and
to-morrow you will do the same to a minister." Then addressing the Duke
of Lennox and the Earl of Mar, who were in the Council, he said, "I am a
Scotchman, my lords, a true Scotchman; and if you are such, take heed
that they do not end with you as they have begun with me."[27] The
King was more disconcerted by this parting shot of Melville's than by
anything that had happened at the interview.

[Note 27: ***Ambassades de M. de la Boderie***, quoted by M'Crie, p.
271.]

On 6th May, Melville's colleagues learned the fate the King had decreed
for them. James Melville was commanded to leave London and go into ward
at Newcastle-on-Tyne; the other six were to return to Scotland to be

confined in districts named in the King's warrant, and they were excluded from any share in the business of the Church courts.

When the others took their journey northwards, James Melville and William Scott remained in London for a fortnight to make arrangements, if possible, to mitigate the imprisonment of their Chief. James Melville, through the indulgence of one of the warders, saw his uncle at the window of his prison for a short time each day during this interval, and permission was obtained for Melville's servant to wait upon him in the Tower; but no other favour was granted. James Melville used every means to gain permission to stay in London and attend to his uncle's comfort, but in vain; and with a sore heart he had to make up his mind to leave him. On the day he and Scott were setting out for the north, two or three of their acquaintances in London visited them; and one of these, a Mr. Corsbie, 'a guid brother, apothecarie of calling,' brought with him 'a great bag of monie alse meikle as he could weill carie in his oxter.' The money had been raised by friends in the city who had been touched by the noble bearing of the ministers before the King and Council, to defray the expenses of their journey as well as the outlay incurred during their residence in London, which the King, with unspeakable meanness, had failed to discharge. This gift the two brethren courteously and gratefully declined. Since James's accession to the English Throne there had been a great outcry against the Scots on account of the beggarly rabble who crossed the Tweed and came to Court to importune the King for 'auld debts' due to them by his Majesty; and Melville and his colleague were resolved that they would furnish the English people with another and a truer version of the character of their countrymen by leaving London poorer than when they came to it. Besides, there were many among the Puritan clergy in the English Church who had been cast out of their livings, and had more need of the money: instead of taking the help offered, the two brethren would rather endeavour to raise money in their own country, poor as it was, to relieve the necessities of these ministers. Their friends gave warm expression to their sense of the honourable motives which led Melville and Scott to decline the gift; and accompanying them to the Tower steps, where the boat was lying that was to convey them to their ship, they bade them affectionate farewell. As the two were rowed down the Thames, they cast many a wistful look back to the prison where they were leaving their beloved friend and Chief at the mercy of a graceless tyrant. And so ended one of the most picturesque and honourable passages in the history of the Scottish Church.

CHAPTER X

THE KING'S ASSEMBLIES

'Gold?   .   .   .   .   .   .

    .   .   .   .

Ha, you gods!   .   .   .   Why, this
Will lug your priests and servants from your sides.'

Timon of Athens.

Before we go on to the closing chapter of Melville's personal history, we must glance at the course of events in Scotland from the time he and his brethren were called to London, up to the Glasgow Assembly in 1610, when the Church made a total surrender to the King, and 'Jericho was buildit up againe in Scotland.'

The Invincibles of the Church having been put out of the way by imprisonment or banishment, the King felt that he might safely call an Assembly to execute his wishes, and to ratify in the Church's name the

restoration of Episcopacy as it had been decreed by the Parliament. So
in the beginning of December 1606, the Assembly was summoned to meet in
Linlithgow. Letters were sent by the King to every presbytery; and they
not only intimated the meeting, but named the representatives to be
sent. In the event of the presbyteries refusing to return the King's
nominees, these were instructed to appear without any presbyterial
mandate. The business was stated to be the suppression of Popery and the
healing of the jars of the Church. In this programme the former item was
the gilt on the pill of the latter. James Balfour--who was in London at
the time--exposed the real character of the Assembly's business when he
was told of it by Bishop Law of Orkney, who had come to Court to report
the proceedings to the King: "'***In nomine Domini incipit omne malum!***
This is pretendit bot the dint will lycht on the Kirk ..."--"They sall
call me a false knave," replied the Bishop, "and never to be believit
again, if the Papists be not sa handleit as they wer never in
Scotland."--"That may weill be,'" was Balfour's rejoinder.

When the House came to the matter which was the real occasion for the
Assembly being held, the question was put, What was the cause of the
jars of the Kirk? And the answer given was, The want of a free Assembly.
King's men as they were, the members had not yet been tamed to entire
servility; as was further shown by their agreeing to petition James on
behalf of the banished ministers, and by their appointing another
Assembly to be held in Edinburgh in the following year. The King's
Commissioner--the Earl of Dunbar--was surely in a compliant mood when he
allowed the House such liberty! But at this point the trump card he had
been concealing in his sleeve was thrown on the table. He proposed in
the King's name that until the business for which the Assembly had been
called was settled, ***Constant*** Moderators should be appointed for the
presbyteries. As it was said at the time, these Constant Moderators were
to be thrust like little thieves into the windows to open the door to
the great thieves--the bishops. Strong objection was made to this fatal
innovation on Presbytery, and it was agreed to, only after cautions,

proposed by the House, had been accepted by the Commissioner.

That even such a tame Assembly was indisposed to yield up the liberties of the Church at the demand of the King was shown by the passing of resolutions intended to clip the wings of the bishops. These resolutions declared, with the concurrence of the bishops themselves, that they were subject to the discipline of the Church and amenable to their own presbyteries.

The King was mightily displeased with his friends in the Assembly because they had not 'proceedit frielyer'; he was enraged at the bishops for submitting themselves to the courts of the Church. The Moderator, Nicolson, Bishop of Dunkeld, at one time James Melville's bosom friend and a standard-bearer of the Kirk, took the King's displeasure so much to heart that he fell ill, and when it was proposed to send for a doctor, replied, 'Send for King James; it is the digesting of his Bishoprick that has wracked my stomack.'

The presbyteries rose up in arms against the Constant Moderators, as did all the synods except Angus; and many scenes of violence took place at the meetings, of these courts through the attempt made by the King's Commissioner to force the adoption of the Acts of the Linlithgow Assembly. The King had still some hard work to do before he could accomplish his purposes. His next step was to propose a conference of ministers, chosen from both sides of the House, to confer on the questions at issue; and meanwhile all public discussion on these questions was to be suspended. The ministers accepted the proposal--another of these fatal concessions by which they were only drawn further into the King's net. Confer and discuss as they might, the King remained the final arbiter, and only one conclusion would be accepted by him. By the suspension of hostilities between the two parties in the Church, those who were opposed to the King gained nothing, and he gained much. While the ministers were silent and

inactive, the bishops were as aggressive as ever; they openly avowed
their intention of conforming the Church to Episcopacy; and they brought
down from London the King's Commissioner and several dignitaries of the
English Church to assist them in the task.

At the next meeting of Parliament, July 1609, the only measure now
needed, so far as Parliament was concerned, to restore a full-blown
Episcopacy, was passed without opposition. There was no minister
present; while Episcopal dignitaries were again brought from London to
grace the proceedings and witness the surrender that was to be made to
their own ecclesiastical polity. At that Parliament 'thai rayd royallie
and Prelat lyk.' The measures that were passed restored the judicial
power of the bishops, their seats in the Court of Session, and their
lands and revenues. Authority was given to them to fix stipends and to
raise or lower them as they were minded, and so the ministers were made
to a large extent their dependants. One of the measures, the setting up
of a High Court of Commission, raised the bishops to a higher degree of
authority than they had ever possessed before. It was virtually a
bishop's court, and it was invested with extraordinary power; those who
sat in it could call before them any person in the kingdom who had
incurred their displeasure, and judge and punish him without law and
without appeal.

The Acts of this Parliament were the King's penultimate stroke against
Presbytery. They armed the bishops with such power, that the King felt
he might at length summon an Assembly which would make submission to
Episcopacy. An Assembly was accordingly held in Glasgow in June 1610;
and there the King's resolutions were carried with only two dissentient
voices. The House was again filled with the King's nominees; and bribes
were distributed among the members to the tune of 40,000 merks. The
bribes were paid in 'Angel' pieces, and so the Assembly came to be known
as the Angelical Assembly. It was money that did the King's 'turn';
'and sa at are stollen dint[28] in are day was overthrown are worke

seventie yeiris in building, and above twenty-four yeiris spacious and most profitabill standing.'

[Note 28: Stolen opportunity.]

CHAPTER XI

THE TOWER: SEDAN

'Here spirits that have run their race, and fought,
And won the fight, and have not fear'd the frowns
Nor lov'd the smiles of greatness, but have wrought
Their Master's will, meet to receive their Crowns.'

HENRY VAUGHAN.

For the first year, Melville's imprisonment was of rigorous severity. The King seemed incapable of any spark of chivalry towards one of the very brightest spirits of his people. James, perhaps least of all the Stuarts, illustrated the principle of *noblesse oblige*. Melville's attendant was taken from him; no visitors were admitted; neither was the use of writing materials allowed. After twelve months, however, some relaxation was gained, through the good offices of Sir James Sempill of Beltrees, the Balladist, who was a warm friend of Melville, and sympathised with him in his struggle to maintain Presbyterianism, although he himself had been brought up at Court--his mother having been maid-in-honour to Queen Mary--and educated along with the King under George Buchanan. He was transferred to a comfortable room in the Tower:

he was now permitted to see friends, and also to write. It was in literary labour he occupied his time. He wrote at least one controversial pamphlet, a reply to a Defence of Episcopacy written by a dignitary of the English Church, and circulated ***gratis*** in Scotland among the ministers; he also translated many of the Psalms. It was in poetical composition, however, that he found his chief recreation and solace. When he quitted the apartment in which he was first confined, the walls were found covered with verses written by him in finely formed characters with the tongue of his shoe-buckle. Every letter he sent to James Melville contained a number of verses 'warm from the anvil.' His nephew, in one of his letters enclosing a remittance of money, had remarked: 'I shall send you money, and you shall send me songs. I have good hope that you will run short of verses for my use before I run short of gold for yours,' to which he replied: 'So you have the confidence to say that the fountain of the Muses from which I draw will be exhausted sooner than the vein of that gold mine, whence you extract the treasures with which you supply me so liberally. Hold, prithee! take care what you say, especially to poets like me, who when I do sing, sing at the invitation of the Muses and under their inspiration.' One of his compositions did not owe its origin to 'the imperative breath of song'; it was an ode to the King, written on the advice of friends, in the hope that such an appeal to his better nature might lead James to grant him his liberty. The ode failed of its purpose; and Melville might have applied to the King with curious fitness the words addressed by the Border outlaw in the ballad to the King's grandfather, James V.:

'To seik het water beneith cauld ice,
Surelie it is a greit follie.
I have asked grace at a graceless face,
But there is nane for my men and me.

But had I kenn'd ere I cam frae hame
How thou unkind wadst been to me,

I wad have keepit the Border side
In spite of all thy force and thee.'

Melville did not expect any other result, although he had been told that
the King seemed favourably disposed towards him. He knew his man:
'*Fronti nulla fides*' was, he said, a proverb often in his mind at that
time. Soon after writing this ode to the King, he, for the same purpose,
submitted an apology to the Privy Council for any offence he had given
by the epigram which had cost him his liberty; but it also failed. In
this matter Archbishop Spotswood played a double part, advising Melville
to send the apology, while he and his brother-prelate, Archbishop
Gledstanes, were doing all they could to prevent the King restoring
Melville and the other exiled ministers to liberty. Melville was no more
disappointed with Spotswood's conduct than he had been with the King's:
'*Sed non ego credulus illis*.'

All his trials and long vexations did not dim his hopefulness; of no
man might it be said more truly that he

'Never doubted clouds would break.'

'Away with fear--I will cherish the hope of everything that is cheering
and joyous.... I betake myself to my sacred anchor--"Seek ye first the
Kingdom of God"'--so he wrote from the Tower.

For some time a son of James Melville who bore his uncle's name, and
another nephew, lodged with Melville in the Tower; and he had many
distinguished visitors, such as Isaac Casaubon and Bishop Hall of
Norwich, who were proud to be numbered among his friends. Another
illustrious victim of the King's treachery, one of the many of England's
noblest sons who stepped from the Tower into immortality, Sir Walter
Raleigh, was a fellow-prisoner of Melville. Did they ever meet? We would
give much to know that they did; it would be pleasant to think of so

rare a conjunction of spirits. Melville found his greatest solace, however, in his nephew's devotion. There was no ministry of love which James Melville failed to render to his uncle; and very touching in their tenderness are the letters which passed between the two. He was also much moved by the tokens of remembrance he received from old friends--comrades in the battles of the Church--and from their children. Acknowledging a gift of money which had been partly contributed by a family of a deceased brother in the ministry, he says: 'I received the Spanish and British angels, equalling in number the Apostles, the Graces, and the Elements, with a supernumerary one of the Seraphic order.... I do not rejoice so much in them (although these commutable pieces of money are at present very useful to me) as I do at the renewing of the memory of my deceased friends, and the prospect of our friendship being perpetuated in their posterity, who have given such a favourable presage of future virtue and genuine piety; for what else could have induced them to take such an interest in my affairs at this time? Wherefore I congratulate them, and I rejoice that this favourable opportunity of transmitting friendship inviolate from father to son and grandson has been afforded.'

The only matter on which there was ever a hint of misunderstanding between Melville and his nephew was the latter's second marriage, to which the uncle was at first much opposed. Their correspondence on this subject contains some passages of lively repartee, in which the elder undoubtedly came off second best. 'The chaste father'--so the younger writes--'who reposed in the embraces of Minerva was not to measure others by himself; he was not ashamed to own he was in love; ay, and had he not the highest precedents for the step he was taking--there were Knox, and Craig, and Pont, and who not else of the venerable fathers of the Church!' 'My sweet Melissa' soon won uncle Andro's affection, and many a gift of garments, embroidered by her skilful hands, found its way to the lonely prisoner in the Tower.

At the close of 1610, the English Ambassador at the French Court brought a request from the Duke de Bouillon, a leading French Protestant, to the King that he would give Melville his release, in order that he might go to Sedan to fill the collegiate Chair of Divinity in the University. After some negotiations, in which James showed his old grudging spirit towards his prisoner, the request was granted. But it was not easy for Melville to tear himself away from his native land. Writing to his nephew, he says:--

'I am in a state of suspense as to the course which I ought to take. There is no room for me in Britain on account of pseudo-Episcopacy--no hope of my being allowed to revisit my native country. Our bishops return home after being anointed with the waters of the Thames. Alas, liberty is fled! religion is banished! I have nothing new to write to you, except my hesitation about my banishment. I reflect upon the active life which I spent in my native country during the space of thirty-six years, the idle life which I have been condemned to spend in prison, the reward which I have received from men for my labours, the inconveniences of old age, and other things of a similar kind, taken in connection with the disgraceful bondage of the Church and the base perfidy of men. But in vain: I am still irresolute. Shall I desert my station? Shall I fly from my native country, from my native Church, from my very self? Or, shall I deliver myself up, like a bound quadruped, to the will and pleasure of men? No: sooner than do this, I am resolved, by the grace of God, to endure the greatest extremity. Until my fate is fixed, I cannot be free from anxiety.'

As Melville, however, continued to weigh the invitation to Sedan, it was more and more borne in upon his mind that it was the call of Providence and the fulfilment of a presage of which he had often spoken, that he was destined to confess Christ on a larger theatre; so he decided to accept it, and left for France on 19th April 1611.

There were six Protestant universities in France, and many of their Chairs were held by Scotsmen who had been Melville's students in St. Andrews. In Sedan, an Aberdonian was Principal, and another fellow-countryman filled the Chair of Philosophy. In this retired frontier town of France, the scene in our own day of the crowning disaster to her army which gave the finishing stroke to the Napoleonic dynasty, Melville spent the remainder of his days; and from it he passed away to the land that was 'nativest' to him.

Some months after settling in Sedan, he received a letter from his nephew with all the home news, which was very gloomy. The bishops were now in their glory. 'If they get the Kingdom of Heaven,' so the Chancellor Seaton said of them, 'they must be happy men, for they already reign on earth.' The pulpits were silent: poor nephew James himself was still in exile, sick, with his heart pierced with many wounds, and longing that he had the wings of a dove that he might fly away and be at rest. To this letter Melville replied in a strain of exuberant cheerfulness:--

'Your letter, my dear James, gave me as much pleasure as it is possible for one to receive in these gloomy and evil days. We must not forget the apostolical injunction, "Rejoice always: rejoice in hope." ***Non si male nunc, et olim erit.*** Providence is often pleased to grant prosperity and long impunity to those whom it intends to punish for their crimes, in order that they may feel more severely from the reverse.... It is easy for a wicked man to throw a commonwealth into disorder: God only can restore it. Empires which have been procured by fraud cannot be stable or permanent. Pride and cruelty will meet with a severe, though it may be a late retribution; and, according to the

Hebrew proverb, "When the tale of bricks is doubled, Moses comes." The result of past events is oracular of the future: "In the mount of the Lord it shall be seen." Why, then, exert our ingenuity and labour in adding to our vexation? Away with fearful apprehensions!'

Turning his thoughts to his old friends and neighbours, the exile makes playful inquiries for their welfare:--

'What is the *profound Dreamer* (so I was accustomed to call him when we travelled together in 1584)--what is our Corydon of Haddington about? I know he cannot be idle; has he not brought forth or perfected anything yet, after so many decades of years? *Tempus Atla veniet tua quo spoliabitur arbos.* Let me know if our old friend Wallace has at last become the father of books and bairns? Menalcas of Cupar on the Eden is, I hear, constant; and I hope he will prove vigilant in discharging all the duties of a pastor, and not mutable in his friendships, as too many discover themselves to be in these cloudy days. Salute him in my name; as also Damoetas of Elie, and our friend Dykes, with such others as you know to "hold the beginning of their confidence and the rejoicing of their hope firm to the end." ... We old men daily grow children again, and are ever and anon turning our eyes and thoughts back on our cradles. We praise the past days because we can take little pleasure in the present. Suffer me then to dote; for I am now become pleased with old age, although I have lived so long as to see some things which I could wish never to have seen. I try daily to learn something new, and thus to prevent my old age from becoming listless and inert. I am always doing, or at least attempting to do, something in those studies to which I devoted myself in the younger part of my life. Accept this long epistle from a talkative old man. *Loqui senibus res est gratissima*,

says your favourite Palingenius, the very mention of whose name
gives me new life; for the **regeneration** forms almost the sole
topic of my meditations, and in this do I exercise myself that
I may have my conversation in heaven.'

How keenly Melville felt the cruelty of the Government in driving
himself and his nephew into exile appears in another part of the same
letter:--

'What crime have you committed? What has the monarch now to
dread? Does not the primate sit in triumph--traxitque sub
astra furorem? What is there, then, to hinder you, and me also
(now approaching my seventieth year, and consequently
emeritus), from breathing our native air, and, as a reward of
our toils, being received into the Prytaneum, to spend the
remainder of our lives, without seeking to share the honours
and affluence which we do not envy the pretended bishops? We
have not been a dishonour to the kingdom, and we are allied to
the royal family. [Melville claimed a consanguinity for his
family with the Stuarts through their common extraction from
John of Gaunt.] But let envy do its worst; no prison, no exile,
shall prevent us from confidently expecting the kingdom of
heaven.'

In the following year Melville was greatly cheered by hearing that all
the exiled ministers had refused an offer which the Crown had made to
allow them to return to their country on condition of their making a
submission to Episcopacy; and he wrote expressing his admiration of
their heroism, and assuring them of his continual remembrance: 'I keep
all my friends in my eye; I carry them in my bosom; I commend them to
the God of mercy in my daily prayers.... I do not sink under adversity;
I reserve myself for better days.'

In April 1614 there fell on Melville the heaviest blow his affection ever received--the tidings of his nephew's death. James Melville died well-nigh broken-hearted; he had not been allowed to return to his own country and resume his charge of his poor seafaring folk, nor to join in France the exile who was so endeared to him. On his deathbed, and within a few hours of the end, when one who was beside him asked if he had no desire to recover, he replied, 'No, not for twenty worlds.' His friends asked him to give them some sign that he was at peace, when he repeated the dying words of the martyr Stephen, and so passed away to that country of his own which all his life he had been seeking.

There is no one in the long line of great Scottish Churchmen whose memory deserves more honour than James Melville, or inspires so much affection, so gracious was his spirit, so pure his character, so disinterested his aims. With the solitary exception which we need not name, there was no one in his own day who rendered better or more varied service to the Church and to the country. For many years he was his uncle's right-hand man as a teacher in our two chief Universities; the Church never had a pastor who had more of the true pastor's heart, nor a leader of more wisdom in counsel, more persuasiveness in conference, more decision in action; it never had a more vivid historian, nor one whose writings are so great a treasure of our Scottish literature. When James Melville came to his grave, how different the world would be to his great kinsman, who could so truly have said, 'Very pleasant hast thou been unto me: thy love to me was wonderful, passing the love of women.' His uncle's grief found its only solace in the thought that he was 'now out of all doubt and fashrie, enjoying the fruits of his suffering here.'

Melville himself never lost his hopefulness and happy ardour. In 1612 he wrote to Robert Durie, one of the banished brethren:--

'Am I not threescore and eight years old; unto the which age

none of my fourteen brethren came? And yet, I thank God, I eat,
I drink, I sleep, as well as I did these thirty years bygone,
and better than when I was younger--in ipso flore
adolescentiae. Only the gravel now and then seasons my mirth
with some little pain, which I have felt only since the
beginning of March the last year, a month before my deliverance
from prison. I feel, thank God, no abatement of the alacrity
and ardour of my mind for the propagation of the truth. Neither
use I spectacles now more than ever, yea, I use none at all,
nor ever did, and see now to read Hebrew without points, and in
the smallest characters. Why may I not live to see a changement
to the better, when the Prince shall be informed truly by
honest men, or God open His eyes and move His heart to see the
pride of stately prelates?'

The last production from Melville's pen was a pamphlet against the
Anglican ceremonies imposed by the King on the Church in The Five
Articles of Perth in 1618. We know little of the last years of his
life. His health apparently gave way in 1620, and he died in Sedan in
1622, having reached his seventy-seventh year.

The only fault Melville's enemies could find with his personal character
was his impetuous and explosive temper. In regard to this, he was his
own best apologist when he said, 'If my anger is from below, trample
upon it; but if from above, let it rise!' If he was 'zealously
affected,' it was always 'in a good thing.' No one could ever charge him
with personal or narrow ambitions. It was always, as he once wrote, his
own desire 'to be concealed in the crowd even when the field of honour
appeared to ripen' before him; and his nephew says of him: 'Whowbeit he
was verie hat in all questiones, yet when it twitched his
particular,[29] no man could crab him, contrare to the common custome.'
No one of braver spirit or truer mould has been among us, and we need to
allow but little for the colouring of affection to accept James

Melville's judgment: 'Scotland never receavit a graitter benefit at the hands of God than this man.' He is one of those great personalities of our history who have left us an example of the moral daring which is the greatest property of the human soul, and the spring of its noblest achievements. The struggle for the advancement of human wellbeing is carried on in ever-changing lines; the problems of the Church and the nation alter; the battlegrounds of freedom and progress shift; but this spiritual intrepidity and scorn of consequence ever remains the chief and most indispensable factor in the highest service of mankind. It is to men like Melville, who have a higher patriotism than that which is bounded by any earthly territory, whose country is the realm of Truth, whose loyalty transcends submission to any human sovereign, that every people owes its noblest heritage. Such are the men who have been the makers of Scotland. '***Sic fortis Etruria crevit***.'

[Note 29: When it concerned his private interest.]

The Codes Of Hammurabi And Moses
W. W. Davies

QTY

The discovery of the Hammurabi Code is one of the greatest achievements of archaeology, and is of paramount interest, not only to the student of the Bible, but also to all those interested in ancient history...

Religion   **ISBN:** *1-59462-338-4*   **Pages:132**
MSRP *$12.95*

The Theory of Moral Sentiments
Adam Smith

QTY

This work from 1749. contains original theories of conscience amd moral judgment and it is the foundation for systemof morals.

Philosophy **ISBN:** *1-59462-777-0*   **Pages:536**
MSRP *$19.95*

Jessica's First Prayer
Hesba Stretton

QTY

In a screened and secluded corner of one of the many railway-bridges which span the streets of London there could be seen a few years ago, from five o'clock every morning until half past eight, a tidily set-out coffee-stall, consisting of a trestle and board, upon which stood two large tin cans, with a small fire of charcoal burning under each so as to keep the coffee boiling during the early hours of the morning when the work-people were thronging into the city on their way to their daily toil...

Pages:84

Childrens   **ISBN:** *1-59462-373-2*   **MSRP** *$9.95*

My Life and Work
Henry Ford

QTY

Henry Ford revolutionized the world with his implementation of mass production for the Model T automobile. Gain valuable business insight into his life and work with his own auto-biography... "We have only started on our development of our country we have not as yet, with all our talk of wonderful progress, done more than scratch the surface. The progress has been wonderful enough but..."

Pages:300

Biographies/   **ISBN:** *1-59462-198-5*   **MSRP** *$21.95*

The Art of Cross-Examination
Francis Wellman

QTY

I presume it is the experience of every author, after his first book is published upon an important subject, to be almost overwhelmed with a wealth of ideas and illustrations which could readily have been included in his book, and which to his own mind, at least, seem to make a second edition inevitable. Such certainly was the case with me; and when the first edition had reached its sixth impression in five months, I rejoiced to learn that it seemed to my publishers that the book had met with a sufficiently favorable reception to justify a second and considerably enlarged edition. ..

Pages:412

Reference   ISBN: *1-59462-647-2*   *MSRP $19.95*

On the Duty of Civil Disobedience
Henry David Thoreau

QTY

Thoreau wrote his famous essay, On the Duty of Civil Disobedience, as a protest against an unjust but popular war and the immoral but popular institution of slave-owning. He did more than write—he declined to pay his taxes, and was hauled off to gaol in consequence. Who can say how much this refusal of his hastened the end of the war and of slavery ?

Law   ISBN: *1-59462-747-9*   **Pages:48**   *MSRP $7.45*

Dream Psychology Psychoanalysis for Beginners
Sigmund Freud

QTY

Sigmund Freud, born Sigismund Schlomo Freud (May 6, 1856 - September 23, 1939), was a Jewish-Austrian neurologist and psychiatrist who co-founded the psychoanalytic school of psychology. Freud is best known for his theories of the unconscious mind, especially involving the mechanism of repression; his redefinition of sexual desire as mobile and directed towards a wide variety of objects; and his therapeutic techniques, especially his understanding of transference in the therapeutic relationship and the presumed value of dreams as sources of insight into unconscious desires.

Pages:196

Dream Psychology
Psychoanalysis for Beginners

Sigmund Freud

Psychology   ISBN: *1-59462-905-6*   *MSRP $15.45*

The Miracle of Right Thought
Orison Swett Marden

QTY

Believe with all of your heart that you will do what you were made to do. When the mind has once formed the habit of holding cheerful, happy, prosperous pictures, it will not be easy to form the opposite habit. It does not matter how improbable or how far away this realization may see, or how dark the prospects may be, if we visualize them as best we can, as vividly as possible, hold tenaciously to them and vigorously struggle to attain them, they will gradually become actualized, realized in the life. But a desire, a longing without endeavor, a yearning abandoned or held indifferently will vanish without realization.

Pages:360

Self Help   ISBN: *1-59462-644-8*   *MSRP $25.45*

The Rosicrucian Cosmo-Conception Mystic Christianity *by Max Heindel*   ISBN: *1-59462-188-8*   **$38.95**
The Rosicrucian Cosmo-conception is not dogmatic, neither does it appeal to any other authority than the reason of the student. It is: not controversial, but is: sent forth in the, hope that it may help to clear...   New Age/Religion Pages 646

Abandonment To Divine Providence *by Jean-Pierre de Caussade*   ISBN: *1-59462-228-0*   **$25.95**
"The Rev. Jean Pierre de Caussade was one of the most remarkable spiritual writers of the Society of Jesus in France in the 18th Century. His death took place at Toulouse in 1751. His works have gone through many editions and have been republished...   Inspirational/Religion Pages 400

Mental Chemistry *by Charles Haanel*   ISBN: *1-59462-192-6*   **$23.95**
Mental Chemistry allows the change of material conditions by combining and appropriately utilizing the power of the mind. Much like applied chemistry creates something new and unique out of careful combinations of chemicals the mastery of mental chemistry...   New Age Pages 354

The Letters of Robert Browning and Elizabeth Barret Barrett 1845-1846 vol II   ISBN: *1-59462-193-4*   **$35.95**
by Robert Browning and Elizabeth Barrett   Biographies Pages 596

Gleanings In Genesis (volume I) *by Arthur W. Pink*   ISBN: *1-59462-130-6*   **$27.45**
Appropriately has Genesis been termed "the seed plot of the Bible" for in it we have, in germ form, almost all of the great doctrines which are afterwards fully developed in the books of Scripture which follow...   Religion/Inspirational Pages 420

The Master Key *by L. W. de Laurence*   ISBN: *1-59462-001-6*   **$30.95**
In no branch of human knowledge has there been a more lively increase of the spirit of research during the past few years than in the study of Psychology, Concentration and Mental Discipline. The requests for authentic lessons in Thought Control, Mental Discipline and...   New Age/Business Pages 422

The Lesser Key Of Solomon Goetia *by L. W. de Laurence*   ISBN: *1-59462-092-X*   **$9.95**
This translation of the first book of the "Lernegton" which is now for the first time made accessible to students of Talismanic Magic was done, after careful collation and edition, from numerous Ancient Manuscripts in Hebrew, Latin, and French...   New Age/Occult Pages 92

Rubaiyat Of Omar Khayyam *by Edward Fitzgerald*   ISBN:*1-59462-332-5*   **$13.95**
Edward Fitzgerald, whom the world has already learned, in spite of his own efforts to remain within the shadow of anonymity, to look upon as one of the rarest poets of the century, was born at Bredfield, in Suffolk, on the 31st of March, 1809. He was the third son of John Purcell...   Music Pages 172

Ancient Law *by Henry Maine*   ISBN: *1-59462-128-4*   **$29.95**
The chief object of the following pages is to indicate some of the earliest ideas of mankind, as they are reflected in Ancient Law, and to point out the relation of those ideas to modern thought.   Religion/History Pages 452

Far-Away Stories *by William J. Locke*   ISBN: *1-59462-129-2*   **$19.45**
"Good wine needs no bush, but a collection of mixed vintages does. And this book is just such a collection. Some of the stories I do not want to remain buried for ever in the museum files of dead magazine-numbers an author's not unpardonable vanity..."   Fiction Pages 272

Life of David Crockett *by David Crockett*   ISBN: *1-59462-250-7*   **$27.45**
"Colonel David Crockett was one of the most remarkable men of the times in which he lived. Born in humble life, but gifted with a strong will, an indomitable courage, and unremitting perseverance...   Biographies/New Age Pages 424

Lip-Reading *by Edward Nitchie*   ISBN: *1-59462-206-X*   **$25.95**
Edward B. Nitchie, founder of the New York School for the Hard of Hearing, now the Nitchie School of Lip-Reading, Inc, wrote "LIP-READING Principles and Practice". The development and perfecting of this meritorious work on lip-reading was an undertaking...   How-to Pages 400

A Handbook of Suggestive Therapeutics, Applied Hypnotism, Psychic Science   ISBN: *1-59462-214-0*   **$24.95**
by Henry Munro   Health/New Age/Health/Self-help Pages 376

A Doll's House: and Two Other Plays *by Henrik Ibsen*   ISBN: *1-59462-112-8*   **$19.95**
Henrik Ibsen created this classic when in revolutionary 1848 Rome. Introducing some striking concepts in playwriting for the realist genre, this play has been studied the world over.   Fiction/Classics/Plays 308

The Light of Asia *by sir Edwin Arnold*   ISBN: *1-59462-204-3*   **$13.95**
In this poetic masterpiece, Edwin Arnold describes the life and teachings of Buddha. The man who was to become known as Buddha to the world was born as Prince Gautama of India but he rejected the worldly riches and abandoned the reigns of power when...   Religion/History/Biographies Pages 170

The Complete Works of Guy de Maupassant *by Guy de Maupassant*   ISBN: *1-59462-157-8*   **$16.95**
"For days and days, nights and nights, I had dreamed of that first kiss which was to consecrate our engagement, and I knew not on what spot I should put my lips..."   Fiction/Classics Pages 240

The Art of Cross-Examination *by Francis L. Wellman*   ISBN: *1-59462-309-0*   **$26.95**
Written by a renowned trial lawyer, Wellman imparts his experience and uses case studies to explain how to use psychology to extract desired information through questioning.   How-to/Science/Reference Pages 408

Answered or Unanswered? *by Louisa Vaughan*   ISBN: *1-59462-248-5*   **$10.95**
Miracles of Faith in China   Religion Pages 112

The Edinburgh Lectures on Mental Science (1909) *by Thomas*   ISBN: *1-59462-008-3*   **$11.95**
This book contains the substance of a course of lectures recently given by the writer in the Queen Street Hall, Edinburgh. Its purpose is to indicate the Natural Principles governing the relation between Mental Action and Material Conditions...   New Age/Psychology Pages 148

Ayesha *by H. Rider Haggard*   ISBN: *1-59462-301-5*   **$24.95**
Verily and indeed it is the unexpected that happens! Probably if there was one person upon the earth from whom the Editor of this, and of a certain previous history, did not expect to hear again...   Classics Pages 380

Ayala's Angel *by Anthony Trollope*   ISBN: *1-59462-352-X*   **$29.95**
The two girls were both pretty, but Lucy who was twenty-one who supposed to be simple and comparatively unattractive, whereas Ayala was credited, as her Bombwhat romantic name might show, with poetic charm and a taste for romance. Ayala when her father died was nineteen...   Fiction Pages 484

The American Commonwealth *by James Bryce*   ISBN: *1-59462-286-8*   **$34.45**
An interpretation of American democratic political theory. It examines political mechanics and society from the perspective of Scotsman James Bryce   Politics Pages 572

Stories of the Pilgrims *by Margaret P. Pumphrey*   ISBN: *1-59462-116-0*   **$17.95**
This book explores pilgrims religious oppression in England as well as their escape to Holland and eventual crossing to America on the Mayflower, and their early days in New England...   History Pages 268

QTY

The Fasting Cure *by Sinclair Upton*   ISBN: *1-59462-222-1* **$13.95**
In the Cosmopolitan Magazine for May, 1910, and in the Contemporary Review (London) for April, 1910, I published an article dealing with my experi-
ences in fasting. I have written a great many magazine articles, but never one which attracted so much attention... New Age/Self Help/Health Pages 164

Hebrew Astrology *by Sepharial*   ISBN: *1-59462-308-2* **$13.45**
In these days of advanced thinking it is a matter of common observation that we have left many of the old landmarks behind and that we are now pressing
forward to greater heights and to a wider horizon than that which represented the mind-content of our progenitors... Astrology Pages 144

Thought Vibration or The Law of Attraction in the Thought World   ISBN: *1-59462-127-6* **$12.95**

by William Walker Atkinson   Psychology/Religion Pages 144

Optimism *by Helen Keller*   ISBN: *1-59462-108-X* **$15.95**
Helen Keller was blind, deaf, and mute since 19 months old, yet famously learned how to overcome these handicaps, communicate with the world, and
spread her lectures promoting optimism. An inspiring read for everyone... Biographies/Inspirational Pages 84

Sara Crewe *by Frances Burnett*   ISBN: *1-59462-360-0* **$9.45**
In the first place, Miss Minchin lived in London. Her home was a large, dull, tall one, in a large, dull square, where all the houses were alike, and all the
sparrows were alike, and where all the door-knockers made the same heavy sound... Childrens/Classic Pages 88

The Autobiography of Benjamin Franklin *by Benjamin Franklin*   ISBN: *1-59462-135-7* **$24.95**
The Autobiography of Benjamin Franklin has probably been more extensively read than any other American historical work, and no other book of its kind
has had such ups and downs of fortune. Franklin lived for many years in England, where he was agent... Biographies/History Pages 332

Name	
Email	
Telephone	
Address	
City, State ZIP	

☐ **Credit Card**   ☐ **Check / Money Order**

Credit Card Number	
Expiration Date	
Signature	

Please Mail to: Book Jungle
PO Box 2226
Champaign, IL 61825
or Fax to: 630-214-0564

ORDERING INFORMATION

web: *www.bookjungle.com*
email: *sales@bookjungle.com*
fax: *630-214-0564*
mail: *Book Jungle PO Box 2226 Champaign, IL 61825*
or PayPal *to sales@bookjungle.com*

Please contact us for bulk discounts

DIRECT-ORDER TERMS

**20% Discount if You Order
Two or More Books**
Free Domestic Shipping!
Accepted: Master Card, Visa,
Discover, American Express